Tidbits

A Fictional Miscellany

Rori Bleu

Rosie Chapel

First printing: 2025
ISBN: 978-1-7637753-4-3 (ebook)
ISBN: 978-1-7637753-5-0 (paperback)

Ulfire Pty. Ltd.
P.O. Box 1481
South Perth
WA 6951
Australia

Cover Design: Rebecca Norman
Images Courtesy: Canva.
Designed in Canva using appropriate licences.

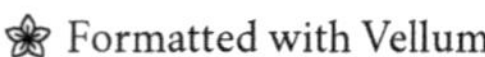 Formatted with Vellum

Tidbits

Dare you take a *bite?*

Dust and Vengeance

Chapter 1

Two men faced each other in the sweltering midday heat.

With the eyes of the citizens of Fortune burning into him as savagely as the rays above, the younger of the pair sweated profusely.

A dust devil swirled up between them.

The younger gunslinger's gaze narrowed on the man at the opposite end of the street. He reckoned he could outdraw the half-breed, a moment for which he had practiced his entire life but, the longer his opponent stood motionless, the less certain he became.

Without warning, the bell in the church tower clanged. Both men went for their pistols. The younger man never got the chance to clear his holster as two .45 caliber slugs tore through his chest.

The victor shoved his pistols into their holsters and turned from his latest kill which would, eventually, be marked by a neat groove etched into his pistol grip.

Several townsfolk of Fortune who had hung around, swarmed the corpse for whatever they could find in the dead man's pockets, including his nickel-finished pistol. The tussle for which saw a few broken noses and eye gouges.

The arrival of the undertaker chased away the vultures before additional customers ended up in his tender care.

The only one among the group who did not seek financial gain from the loser lying face down in the street was a broad-shouldered man wearing what looked like his Sunday best, complete with derby, smoking a fat cigar, and observing the mortician practice his profession.

His sophisticated attire did little to camouflage his heartless nature.

The town of Fortune was once exactly what its name implied. Prospectors were drawn to the town, located in the heart of the Arizona Territory, seeking riches in the form of silver. Soon, much to the consternation and ire of the local Apache tribes, claims dotted their sacred Superstition Mountains, which surrounded the settlement.

Even with the inevitable skirmishes between the Apache and the miners, there was more than enough of the shiny metal to make everyone rich.

Until Uriah Black came to town.

Employing unsavory tactics, he consolidated a vast majority of the claims under his ownership, including Silverstock, the largest producing mine, which he renamed the Black Burrows Mine, coincidentally, the only mine serviced directly by the Black Rock Railway.

By bribing the various territory politicians, Black was awarded the private spur between Fortune and Phoenix and beyond to the Union Pacific lines. Any of the independent mines not under his control were charged an exorbitant fee to transport their payload to market.

It did not take long for the city's resources to run dry, forcing desperate men to take desperate measures just to survive.

Flushed with success at gaining these two elements in his aim to control the town, Black set his sights on the bar and gambling halls. While taking over the smaller joints had proved easy, the jewel of Fortune lay beyond his grasp.

Mainly because of the gun the woman who owned the place had hired.

He grew irritated at throwing good money after bad, bringing these self-proclaimed quick draws to town to rid Fortune of anyone who dared stand in his way and, in particular, the Faro dealer at *Belle's Saloon.*

It was time he took matters into his own hands.

Crushing the cigar under his boot, he headed toward the telegraph office.

Several Days Later

The tall, slender man dressing in the midmorning light was named Gian-nah-tah, after his people's great chief, by his Apache mother who hoped this would encourage her tribe to accept him as a member. He was the result of her rape by a gang of bandoleros.

Her chin bore the stripes tattooed by her tribe representing each man who abused her, after which, none of her peoples' warriors would touch her.

Among the Mexicans who populated the town he now called home, he was known as *El Portador de la Muerte,* the Bringer of Death.

For the white settlers, he had adopted the name of Rafe Skye

His admirers swore the ambidextrous gunslinger was blessed by the good Lord, and those who wished he had never shown his face in town, pledged he was a product of Hell itself.

His hair braided, he stared into the mirror, remembering the dozen or so fools who had tried and failed to make a name for themselves by venturing into Belle's Saloon, looking for the half-breed who ran the Faro table, demanding a showdown.

Every duel was reduced to a notch on one of the wooden grips of his twin, blue-finished, Colt Single Action Army pistols. A habit he had begun at the death of a certain army officer.

The tools of his trade were trophies from the ongoing Apache Wars with the United States government.

He was part of a warring party who thwarted a raid on his village by the US Cavalry. The fat sergeant, from whom he took the guns — despite such things being taboo for an Apache warrior for fear of angering the dead — also lost a good chunk of his scalp, which now adorned his wall.

No matter how skilled they thought they were, the result never changed. The dusty road leading to the cemetery ended up stained with bloodied tracks as the undertaker dragged the bodies to their last resting place.

Today felt different, something was off. Rafe was beset by an unidentifiable uneasiness, prompting him to double check his trusty six shooters were loaded and at the ready as he tucked them into his cross holsters.

He settled his broad-brimmed hat on his head, consigning any reservations to the far recesses of his mind. He smiled at his reflection, and reassured himself it was just another day.

Chapter 2

Coming out of his room, Rafe greeted a couple of the 'barmaids', Belle kept on the payroll, with a tip of his hat. The pair giggled as he passed. For the life of him, he could never remember either serving a drink to any of the customers, though the regulars spent plenty of silver buying *them* shots.

After descending the stairs, he paused at the oak bar. Jesse, the barman, was busy polishing the wood in preparation for the nightly troublemakers.

"Hey, Jesse, is the boss in?"

Without looking up, the barman smirked. "Can't say, though I'd love to see those sweet cheeks of hers walk by."

"Not even in your dreams, Jesse." A throaty chuckle came from the door to an adjacent office. The tap of boots crossing the wooden floor penetrated the relative quiet of the empty saloon. The girls loitering on the gallery above called out a friendly greeting to the petite, dark-haired beauty as she appeared from a dim corridor and approached her card sharp.

Rafe smiled and nodded to the woman who, despite her

diminutive stature, exuded confidence. "Glad to see you could join us peasants early, boss."

Belle McGantt, owner of the saloon which bore her name, winked at the dealer, and returned the smile. "Hush your mouth, Rafe. I've been working all morning to ensure you and the girls get paid."

"Hey," Jesse chimed in. "What about me?"

"You, my friend, are working off the booze you sneak *every* night. Don't think I don't know what you're up to."

"Women," was all Jesse offered as a rebuttal.

Returning her attention to Rafe, she addressed an issue weighing heavily on her since she had found out the previous night.

"I need you to be observant this evening, Rafe."

"Such a big word from such a small woman." He chuckled.

"Shut up and listen. A gang of Black's miners are supposed to be in town tonight. They'll no doubt be liquored up by the time they reach us. So, be prepared for anything."

"Aye, aye, boss," Rafe acknowledged. "Oh, and if you don't mind me saying, you're looking as pretty as a royal flush."

As ever, his compliment elicited a fiery blush. Ignoring it, Belle confined herself to a lofty, "Behave yourself and get to work."

She hated herself for putting him in the position of risking his life for her, and that she had not possessed the courage to explain his duties fully when she offered him the job.

Grasping the doorknob to her office, Belle shot Rafe a speculative glance, ruminating over whether to tell him about Black's unwelcome proposal in relation to the saloon.

Settling into his customary table, Rafe shuffled a new deck of cards. Everyone in town knew the games at Belle's Saloon were fair and honest.

Even though Rafe was taught by the best of the cardsharps, no one could accuse him of dealing from the bottom of the deck, like they did down the street at Santa Rosa's.

While he waited for the first players of the day to show up, he dealt a couple of hands of solitaire. It did not take long from the time Jesse opened the doors for customers to appear at his table.

"Hey, Rafe." Jeremiah Brooks smiled as he pulled his chair up to the table. One of the few independent mine owners left in town, Jeremiah set down a meager stack of silver dollars.

Rafe eyed the coins and asked his friend politely, "You sure you want to sit down?"

"Well, the mine was a little skimpy this week with its offerings, so I figured I'd have a better chance of fleecing you. Ya know how the bank hates being paid late on their notes."

Chuckling, they nodded in agreement, and began playing *Twenty-one*. Jeremiah was the only person with whom Rafe played this particular game. No one else was allowed to participate.

Rafe knew when Jeremiah was short on funds to pay the bank's exorbitant interest rates. He also knew his friend was too proud to ask for help, so they played this game. Rafe threw a couple of hands until he was sure Jeremiah was in better financial shape.

It was an unspoken favor, one Jeremiah never failed to repay when he came into some coin. Belle was aware of their 'game', and respected Rafe's silent support of his friend. Few men possessed such consideration.

Knowing never to offer Jeremiah alcohol, Rafe suggested instead, "You look a little parched. Need some water?"

"Nah, I'm good." Jeremiah studied the hand he was dealt. He tossed a silver dollar on the table to start bidding.

"You sure that pretty wife of yours won't meet you at the door with a frying pan to your head when you lose?"

"Went to Phoenix to visit her folks. She don't know I'm here," Jeremiah reassured Rafe, as he threw down his winning hand.

"Damnit, man," Rafe feigned disappointment. "Looks like Lady Luck is on your side today."

"Just watch me clean ya out."

The two played cards for the next hour or so until Jeremiah smiled and said, "Well, I don't want your boss to blame me for wrecking her profits, so I'll have mercy on you and call it a day."

"Well, don't forget to stop by some time and give me the chance to win it back."

"Yeah, yeah," Jeremiah agreed. "Now, my friend, if you will excuse me, I should get to the bank before they close."

"Be safe and say hello to Sara for me when she gets home."

Jeremiah stood and extended his hand to Rafe who shook it firmly, then watched his friend disappear into the street.

Rafe straightened his table and was opening a new deck of cards for the waiting Faro players when the harsh rumble of angry voices from the street drowned out the buzz of chatter in the saloon. He thought one might be Jeremiah but, in Fortune, arguments in the street were commonplace and could be anybody.

It was the sound of gunfire which propelled him and most of the saloon outside.

In the dry street lay Jeremiah Brooks, face down and motionless. His Colt Union army issued .44 lay next to him.

Certain the two men standing over Jeremiah, muttering in undertones, were employed by Uriah Black, Rafe charged towards them demanding, "What happened?"

The duo looked at each other, and one of them sneered, "This crazy dirt digger drew his gun and tried to hold us up."

Rafe searched his friend's body, discovering the money he had just won, missing.

He glared at the men, defending his friend with an angry, "That's hogwash, and you know it. He had no call to rob anyone, he had more than enough money."

Both shrugged, and the second man scoffed, "I'm guessin' he went crazy from all that silver mine dust them people inhale."

Rage consumed Rafe, and he reached for his pistols, but the other two already had their guns drawn and had the drop on him.

"Whoa there, Geronimo," the first cowboy warned Rafe derisively. "How about you pull those California bulldozers out, butt first, and hand them over. Then we can have a civilized conversation."

Using the great Apache medicine man's name as an insult smarted, but Rafe did not let it show, recognizing these boys were itching for a fight.

He withdrew his pistols, barrels down, grips facing the two men. In a split-second decision, Rafe pulled a move he had practiced but had never tried in real world conditions, the Curly Bill spin, taught to him by none other than Curly Bill Brocius of the Clanton-McLaury Cowboys gang.

He hooked his fingers through the trigger guard of each pistol. Flipping them upside down, he fired at the men. Unable to aim properly, he managed to hit one in his chest, dropping him to the ground next to Jeremiah.

His second shot went wild, missing the other man altogether.

Before the man could return fire, a shot went off into the air behind him. It was Fortune's sheriff, Clifford Baines. A man so deep into Uriah Black's pocket, most of the honest citizens of the town assumed he had built his shack there.

"Wesley, what the hell is goin' on here?" The old man with a bushy, white moustache and beard growled.

The man still standing spun on his heel and declared, theatrically, "Thank God, you're here, Sheriff. This crazy half-breed killed Bobby Grogan for no reason. He just barely missed me."

Baines gave Wesley a hairy eye before looking at Rafe.

"That true, Skye?" Baines did not bother to conceal the animosity he felt toward Rafe.

"That's a lie, Sheriff. Those two murdered Jeremiah in cold blood and robbed him."

"Lies," Wesley barked.

"Shuddup, Wesley," the sheriff ordered, his attention on Rafe. "Ya have any witnesses to back up your claim?"

Rafe looked around at all of those who had gathered around. To a person, each tried their hardest to avoid his eyes.

He had to admit, "Looks like the answer is no."

Baines called out to the crowd, "Did any of you see Skye shoot this man?"

"I did," a grizzled cowboy called out from in front of the mercantile store. "Grogan didn't stand a chance."

"Christ," the sheriff mumbled. "An' Judge Decauter won't be back around this side of the circuit until the end of next month.

"I don't really have the space or desire to lock ya up until then, Skye."

"Look, Sheriff…" Wesley offered. "I have a better solution. Let me face this killer and put him down like the rabid dog he is. My friend deserves to be avenged."

Rubbing his beard, Baines pretended to give the suggestion serious consideration.

Unbeknownst to either Wesley or Rafe, and even though the latter was the better gunman, Baines' instructions were to agree to the showdown. Black would be furious if he lost another man, but that was *his* problem.

After a protracted moment, the sheriff assented, "Fine, tomorrow at noon. If either of ya dares to skip town, I'll have ya hunted down and hung."

"Don't I get a say?" Rafe asked, though he figured it was a waste of his breath.

"Of course, Injun." Baines jerked his head in the direction of the gibbet. "I can string ya up right now, if ya'd rather."

Chapter 3

The Next Day
11:55 AM

Early, as was his habit, Rafe waited for Wesley under the noon-day sun.

His thoughts drifted to the previous day. Belle had talked herself hoarse in an effort to convince him he should run, insisting that Baines's threat of tracking him down was nothing but hot air.

Justice for Jeremiah, and his personal pride, would not allow him to do so.

Double checking his weapons for the final time, he assured himself they were fully loaded, and the cylinders were spinning freely.

Snapping both pistols closed, their hammers cocked and ready, he put them into their holsters.

A glance at his pocket watch prompted him to question whether time had brought clarity to Wesley regarding the likelihood he was about to lose his life for all the wrong reasons.

At the chime of spurs, Rafe closed his watch, put it back into his pocket, and looked up.

He quashed the urge to laugh when he saw Wesley dressed all in black, as though he was some perverse Grim Reaper, nickel-plated six shooter strapped to his right hip.

"Just as I thought, another hired gun after all," Rafe muttered to himself.

"You ready to die, half-breed?" Wesley taunted.

"One day is just as good as the next," Rafe replied philosophically. "Shall we get to it."

The two stood, frozen in place, hands hovering above their pistols. The next few minutes ticked by as though each was an eternity in the making.

An almost imperceptible click reached Rafe's ears. No one else in the crowd seemed to notice, except Wesley. Whatever the source, it caused the latter to twitch.

Ignoring the caution screaming in his mind, Rafe took his eyes off Wesley, a split second before the noon bell rang out, and did not have time to dodge the shot which tore through him, rupturing his heart.

Rafe slumped to his knees, seeing Wesley shove his pistol into its holster but knew the fatal shot had not come from his opponent's .45. No, it came from somewhere above and behind him.

His vision dimming, Rafe squinted at the top of the bell tower, spying the glint from the barrel perched there.

Rafe Skye's last breath sucked in the dirt from the street as he collapsed, face-first.

Confidently, Wesley strolled to Rafe's corpse, knelt next to the body and liberated the latter's pistols.

"My right for killing you, Skye," he informed the dead man as he stood to leave.

During the War of Northern Aggression, Uriah Black served in Robert E. Lee's Confederate Army of Northern Virginia as a sharpshooter in Rodes' Battalion.

At seventeen, he ran away from his family's farm in Pennsylvania to join the Rebels. Their cause for *States Rights* versus the tyranny of a federally controlled government resonated with him.

His older brother, Tyler, had already joined the 14th Pennsylvania Cavalry Regiment where he had proved himself, even in the disastrous first months of the war, rising to the rank of Captain.

On the sweltering summer day of July 2, 1863, in the town of Gettysburg, Pennsylvania, a ferocious engagement between Southern and Northern soldiers continued to wage from the previous day.

Swaths of land were gained and lost on both sides. As the Confederates were poised to seize territory from the North, Union soldiers fell back in a frantic retreat.

In town, on the upper floor of a house was a sharpshooter's nest. Through the open window, Black saw a Union officer astride a chestnut Morgan mount, trying desperately to regroup the fleeing Union troops. It was a horse he knew well and had helped break as a younger boy.

Taking aim at the soldier's head, he angled the shot just high enough to send the man's hat flying without injuring the wearer.

Instinctively, the man raised his hand to check his head, twisting on his horse to glare in the direction from where he was positive the shot had originated.

In the open window, he saw a Confederate throw him a salute before taking aim at him again. Tyler had no doubt the next shot would be true. He reciprocated in kind, and spurred his horse out of town.

Black never saw his brother after that encounter. Tyler's life was taken during the Battle of Cold Harbor.

As for his current long-distance attempt from Fortune's belltower, Black knew this shot was one any self-respecting sharpshooter would consider an act of cowardice, but it meant he had rid himself of the persistent pain in the ass protecting Belle's Saloon.

Slinging his Whitworth rifle over his shoulder, Black made his way to the ladder leading to the ground floor of the tower.

Chapter 4

Black swaggered into Belle's establishment. He knew the sheriff had no intention of investigating the shot which took Rafe's life. There was no need to, Black had already laid out the scenario.

All eyes in the bar swiveled to the door when he entered. The rifle slung over his shoulder, an unspoken message to Belle about her future.

Making himself comfortable at Rafe's former table, Black called to Jesse, "Barman, a bottle of whiskey from under the bar not that crap behind the counter, and two *clean* shot glasses. I'm celebrating."

At the sound of his voice, Belle burst out of an upstairs room, rattling the door on its hinges.

She stormed down the wooden staircase, her outrage echoing around the saloon, "Get your sorry butt out of my—"

Her words were lost when, insolently, he tossed back his first glass.

"Show some respect and lower your voice, woman." Black shrugged his rifle off his shoulder, laid it on top of the table, and helped himself to another drink.

"Take a seat, Belle. Now."

Belle's troubled gaze slid between the rifle and the man she detested more than the rattlesnakes which occasionally slithered their way into the saloon. Mulishly, she yanked out the indicated chair, and did as Black had bidden.

Pouring a snifter into the second tumbler, Black pushed it across the green baize. "To *our* new partnership." He raised his whiskey.

She picked up her glass and threw its contents in his face. "I do not know where you got that ludicrous notion. This bar is mine and mine alone, and take note, Uriah Black, I saw you in that bell tower right before it rang. I'm gonna have the US Marshall on your neck before you can—"

Running the back of his hand across his wet face, he continued as though she had not interrupted, "For what, my dear woman?" his tone, sugary sweet. "To tell him your half-breed lover was killed in a fair gunfight. Something, I have no doubt, the good Sheriff Baines will corroborate."

"*Fair*?" Belle squawked, ignoring the accusation she was sleeping with Rafe. "*You* shot him, not your hired gun. You staged everything."

"I have no idea what lunacy you're pedaling, Belle. You must be suffering from the vapors. Perhaps you ought to see whether Doc has something for your hysterics. Until you calm down, I suggest you stop sqaunderin' good whiskey. It's hard enough to come by in these parts. Then again, as a former saloon owner—"

"Former?" Belle exclaimed, incredulously, unsure she had heard him correctly.

"Aye, and you'll be wantin' a new watchdog now your Apache is dead and, I'll wager, you're in need of protection." Black stroked the stock of his Whitworth. "Never mind that you're a dealer down."

Rage burned in Belle's eyes. She spat, "Jesse can run the table."

"Leaving who to serve your loyal customers? We both know he consumes an abundance of your profits already."

"I'll have one of *my* girls deal," Belle countered heatedly.

"Riiiiight… because the players in town will trust the games they run," Black drawled.

Aware he had backed Belle into a figurative corner, Black's next words were nothing short of smug. "Tell ya what, how about I get one of Rosa's dealers to take the position. One less thing to worry that pretty little head of yours."

"No way any of those cheatin' bastards will work here."

"I'll also make sure she sends Tommy over—"

"To what? Roll the drunks?"

"Hardly," Black feigned affront at the accusation. "Let's just say to see things run smoothly."

"Is that not *my* job?"

Black swallowed the last mouthful of whiskey. "No, Belle. How about you tend the bar so you can keep track of your bartender. Think of it as a cost-cutting exercise."

With no more to be said, for now, Black shoved back his chair, got to his feet and picked up his rifle. He paused at the door. "Oh, and when I return, we'll talk about your salary and pricing."

Striding out of the saloon, Black all but bowled over a small, mousy woman dressed in black. He had no idea who she was, unaware the woman had no doubt as to his identity.

Tipping his hat, he offered a rare apology, "Beggin' your pardon, ma'am."

The woman gave no absolution for his rudeness. Instead, she harrumphed and walked to the bar.

Unperturbed by her reaction, he shrugged and headed to Santa Rosa's.

Motionless, the woman stood in front of Jesse who had

no idea what to make of her. Finally, he groused in frustration, "Look if you're one of those damned Temperance biddies, take your tambourine and beat it somewhere else."

Setting her jaw, the woman demanded, "I want a shot of the strongest stuff you have, and to talk to your boss."

Jesse knew Belle would beat him to a bloody pulp if he dared serve this woman any of their standard rot gut whiskey. In hopes of saving his tail, he poured her a glass of wine, which was little more than fermented grape juice.

"That'll be two bits, ma'am."

"Start a tab, man and get your employer."

Belle, who had overheard the exchange, appeared before Jesse could summon her.

"I'm Belle, and this is my place," she addressed the woman, adding absently, "Leastways, for the time being. If you are looking for a job, I am not hiring. If you are trying to collect on a debt, you'll have to speak with the new owner. Seems I've been—"

"I am Sara Brooks," the newcomer's abrupt tones told Belle her pleasantries were a waste of breath. "Is what our esteemed sheriff telegraphed about my Jeremiah true? Thankfully, there was a train leaving for Fortune this morning, otherwise, I would be sitting at my sister's fretting about him."

"I'm not sure what that might be, but perhaps we ought to continue this conversation in private."

Chapter 5

Belle ushered Sara into the office, invited her to make herself comfortable on the leather settee, and closed the door.

Crossing to a Regency-style cabinet close to her desk. Belle produced a small silver key hanging on a delicate chain around her neck, and unfastened the ornate lock.

Opening the doors, she frowned at the amount of fine greyish powder which had found its way inside, feeling obliged to apologize to her guest for the coating of dust, "Don't you just hate how the desert gets into everything?"

Sara did not reply. She appeared to have more important things on her mind than house cleaning.

Using her sleeve, Belle wiped two of the tasting glasses, then doing the same with a bottle of Spanish sherry, experiencing a pang in her heart when she saw the label. It was one she had bought in New York as part of her first shipment of alcohol for her newly acquired saloon in the Arizona Territory.

While the rest of the shipment was transported via rail and stagecoach, she had carried this bottle personally.

Intended to be uncorked to salute her opening night it was forgotten when a fistfight broke out between two drunken cowboys. A night when Belle conceded she was not quite prepared for the challenges faced by a woman running a business in the West.

The bottle became something of a symbol to be used when she found a moment to celebrate with the one she loved.

That too had died in Fortune's main street forty-… Belle glanced at the clock… seven minutes ago.

Sighing, she popped the cork and poured the drinks.

"I hope you don't mind sherry." Belle handed Sara a glass, then settled into the chair behind her desk. The realization that, shortly, neither would be hers slid like a shard of ice through her mind.

Crushing the notion, she gave her full attention to the widow perched awkwardly on the low couch, who was downing the expensive sherry with rather more haste than appreciation.

"Now, Sara," Belle started, hoping to slow her down, "what exactly did the sheriff tell you?"

Sara produced a crumpled piece of paper from her satchel and dumped it on the desk, exchanging it for the bottle and a second *taste*, before resuming her seat.

Belle refrained from commenting and unfolded the sheet, smoothing it out to make it easier to read.

The missive was brief. God forbid the town should pay for a more detailed message.

Mrs. Brooks, <Stop>
Your husband was shot in an attempted robbery. <Stop>
Collect his body immediately. <Stop>
Sincerely, Sheriff Clifford Blaines <Stop>

Acknowledging a dead body festered quickly in the Arizona heat, Belle fought to mask her irritation at the sheriff's insensitive choice of words, and said gently, "I am afraid it's true. One of Black's men claimed Jeremiah tried to rob—"

"*Rob?*" the woman scoffed. "Jeremiah would *never* rob anybody. He may have been too proud to ask for help for his own good, but his sense of morality would not allow him to do something as heinous as pull a weapon on *anyone*."

A smile brightened Belle's face as she recalled the last game between Rafe and Jeremiah. "I am aware of the merits of your husband, Sara, and know he had no reason to rob anyone. He cleaned out my dealer—"

Sara burst out into tears, knowing the symbolism of the two men's card games. Stammering, "O-Oh, G-God, I don't h-how I-ll be ever to pay you back. Hopefully, w-when the sheriff r-returns his belongings—"

Belle shook her head, "You'll find no money there. They picked his body clean."

Sara dabbed at her eyes with a snowy white handkerchief, apologizing profusely for the loss of the money.

"W-where is Mr. Skye?" Sara inquired. "I must beg his pardon and thank him for all he has done for Jeremiah."

It was Belle's turn for waterworks. "That will not be necessary. Uriah Black killed Rafe less than an hour ago," she sobbed.

"What? How?" Sara blurted out in shock.

"In a gunfight."

"No one was faster than Rafe Skye. How could that ugly sack of horse dung outshoot him?"

Sara's description of Black caught Belle by surprise and caused her to snort a sniffle. Collecting herself, she retorted, "It was anything but a fair fight. It was an assassination."

"What on earth for?" Sara found this difficult to comprehend. While Black had been after the claim Jeremiah and she owned since the day he arrived in town, killing Rafe made no sense.

"He wants my bar, and Rafe stood in his way," Belle spat.

In the ensuing silence, Belle could almost see the gears grinding in the grieving widow's head.

Sara walked to the window and watched the daily business going on up and down the side street as though a murder had not just occurred.

Without averting her gaze from the scene below she observed, "You plan to roll over and play dead for Uriah Black like everybody else in this Godforsaken town."

"Like hell I will," came Belle's implacable reply.

"Then perhaps the two of us should work together."

As promised, Black returned to the saloon, a couple of his lackeys in tow.

From behind the bar, Belle watched Black direct thug number one — a balding man in a smart shirt, sleeves banded, cuffs buttoned at the wrists, and dusty black trousers — to the Faro table.

She wanted to object to his presence in the dealer's nook, but her attention was drawn to the second and much bigger man filling the door frame.

"Tommy, grab a chair in the corner and stay there until I need you," Black instructed.

Thug number two nodded, grunted a "Mister Black," and chose a spot where he had an unobstructed view of the saloon including the entrance.

Regrettably, the chair he wanted was already occupied by a regular customer.

"Move," Tommy barked.

"Nah, I'm good here. Take that one." The cowboy, his seat

tilted on two legs to rest against a pillar, nodded at an adjacent table.

Without warning, Tommy kicked the chair out from under the man who went sprawling.

The cowboy reached for his pistol, but Tommy was already pointing his Colt at the man's head. "I asked politely the first time. I advise you to leave before the mortician pays you a visit."

Scooping up his hat, the cowboy fled the saloon.

Tommy righted the chair and took his place without saying another word.

Gratified to note Belle had bowed to his edict, Black greeted her with a breezy, "Afternoon, ma'am, you must be the new bartender. I hope you can pour a better drink than your usual booze clerk."

Refusing to rise to the bait, Belle continued to clean the glasses.

"Two items of business of which you should be aware," she replied. "First, the widow Brooks has signed her claim over to me as collateral against the money her husband owed, to be returned to her when the debt is repaid."

This was akin to a Christmas miracle for Black. With Belle under his thumb, it was only a matter of time before he gained access to the title — legally, of course.

"And the second?" he queried.

"She's in the kitchen as *your* new cook."

Black cocked his head in amusement. "This place has a working kitchen to feed these clodhoppers?"

"It was a stage stop before it became a saloon."

"Then why did you not offer food when you took over?"

"I could not find anyone able to cook worth a dime. Besides, if the widow has no source of income, how is she supposed to pay off the debt?"

"That's really not *our* problem, now, is it?"

"Nope, you're right. It's not our problem. It's *yours*. Skye lost a hefty amount of this month's profits."

"Typical," Black growled. "Even dead, he's a headache. Let Brooks know she had better not disappoint, or I'll find other ways for her to pay me back."

"Horse's ass," Belle muttered under breath.

"What was that?"

"I asked if you wanted a glass. You're in charge now."

"Now there's a dandy idea." He addressed the near empty saloon, "New management. Next round is on the house."

Chapter 6

Outwardly, Belle behaved as a dutiful employee and face of the saloon. To her surprise, Black ensured Buck, thug number one, ran a respectable table, for the most part.

Business also increased when word of Sara's delicious cooking spread around the town, generating enough income that Black almost forgot about Sara's silver claim — *almost*.

One evening, while the other employees were closing the saloon for the day, Black summoned Belle into his office, ordering her to, "Close the door behind you."

Inviting her to sit down, he took the half-full bottle of sherry out of the cabinet, the lock to which he had long since jimmied.

Ignoring the smaller glasses, he chose a highball, only bothering to dust the rim before he filled it.

Belle pretended not to notice and accepted the drink.

He pulled a bottle of bourbon out of the desk drawer and poured one for himself, his toast leaving a lot to be desired. "I don't know how you can stomach that crap."

Shrugging indifferently, she swallowed a gritty mouthful.

"While I appreciate you sharing *my* Spanish sherry, so generously, I cannot help but feel there is an ulterior motive for this night cap." Her thinly veiled sarcasm sailed straight over Black's head.

"As observant as ever." He grinned through a gulp of bourbon. "Do you still have control of Brooks's claim?"

"Yes, and it is tucked away safely. Why?"

"I think it would be to the widow's advantage if she sold us her claim outright. Our current profit allows us to offer her a generous sum for the mine. Ample for her to start a new life away from Fortune. Ya know, like San Francisco, maybe."

Belle took another sip. "I haven't heard her say that she wants to leave."

"Because no one has pointed out the benefits. Why don't you take some of that sherry and *convince* her."

Always the bastard, the words ran through her brain. "I cannot promise anything, but I'll sound her out. Is there anything else?"

Black put his glass down, rose and, skirting the desk, planted his backside on the edge of the polished wood in front of Belle. "What if there is something *I* can do for *you*?"

He leant forward to stroke Belle's check. It was all Belle could do, not to retch or recoil, but the gesture was not unexpected, and something for which Sara and she had already prepared.

Steadying herself, she batted her lashes and mustered up her most doe-like expression.

"I-I am not quite sure what you mean, Mr. Black."

"Please, Belle, call me Uriah."

Feigning hesitancy, she stammered, "A-as you wish, U-Uriah."

"The way I see it, if the two of us join forces, not only can we run Fortune, but also control the whole territory."

She tapped her chin with her forefinger, as though considering his words. "An ambitious goal, Uriah, but how?"

"Total trust, my dear, which might also necessitate us becoming... closer." He brushed a kiss to her lips.

Belle felt as though she was signing a pact with the devil. As Black drew back, she forced a smile and an accompanying blush.

"A little something to ponder." Black dipped his head, his mouth curving in satisfaction. "First, let us concentrate on persuading Brooks to sell her claim."

Leaving Black in his office, dreaming of a future with her, Belle went behind the bar to grab the strongest whiskey she could find.

Referred to, fondly, as coffin varnish, guaranteed to heal every ailment, or put you in your grave, she removed the cork, took a slug then spat it out, hoping to rinse the foul taste of Black's kiss from her mouth, then headed to the kitchen so Sara and she could fine-tune their plan.

Perched on the freshly washed butcher's block, Belle... to Sara's well-concealed consternation... continued to drink straight from the bottle, while the former finished her chores.

Sara stopped mopping the floor to admonish, "Do you intend to drink the lot?" Leaning against the mop handle, she stretched out a hand, raising the bottle in a salute when Belle passed it over.

She took a long swig, hiccupped, then noticed the look on Belle's face. "What?"

"Black wants me to sell him your deed," Belle's scathing tone and dramatic eye roll underscored her low opinion of Black's proposal.

"Does he not understand you holding the deed is collateral not ownership?"

"He believes I can convince you otherwise, that you would benefit from the sale." An image of Sara enjoying life away from this unforgiving frontier popped into Belle's mind.

"Is he right?" she murmured, almost as an afterthought.

Sara threw up her hands at Belle's question. "Are you daft in the head?"

"Well, I doubt you're gonna start busting rock for silver. I agree he's vermin, but what if by selling him the claim you could start a new life? Do you want to stay here with all your sad memories? It seems like a fair price, in itself, a rarity."

Sara snorted her derision. "Knowing the man responsible for taking my Jeremiah still draws breath, is bad enough. I could not live with myself if I accepted *anything* from him, let alone money. The very notion makes me sick to my stomach."

"So, we stick to the original plan?"

"Unless you're getting cold feet." Sara shot back, not bothering to dilute the accusation in her voice.

"No, no," Belle assured, quashing her vague misgivings.

Relishing the role of saloon owner, Black sat in on a hand or two of Faro, winning every game, of course. He took the winnings and bought drinks for the gamblers at the table, as well as ensuring the saloon girls were tending to them.

Once Belle handed him the signed deed to the Brooks' Family Mine, he owned yet another profitable silver vein —

legitimately. Furthermore, Black had persuaded Sara to stay on until a replacement could be hired in her stead.

Everything was going the robber baron's way.

Throughout the evening, Belle caught him staring at her with a ridiculously mischievous look, like a little boy with a secret, dying to spill the beans.

Unbeknownst to her, when the saloon closed for the night, Black intended to invite her up to the room he had commandeered, without a by your leave, to cement their partnership once and for all.

The opportunity presented itself when the last of the gamblers cashed out around midnight.

Jesse and Sara began their end of shift clean, but Black chased them off home, stating he would pay them extra to come in earlier than usual the next day to take care of the remaining areas.

Satisfied the saloon was empty, Black crept up behind Belle, slid his arms around her waist, and nuzzled her shoulder. He felt her tremble in his arms, mistaking it for anticipation.

He whispered into her ear, "I have a surprise for you in my office. Have a look and meet me in my room."

Brushing a kiss to the top of her head, Black placed his palm on her back, urging her to the office.

In the light of the single oil lamp, Belle spotted two packages. The first one she guessed was alcohol. Unwrapping it, she found a bottle of wine, whose French-sounding name she could not pronounce.

The Uriah Black she knew was too parsimonious to pay the exorbitant import fees levied on genuine wine for her, and assumed it was a cheap imitation from California.

She was less sure about the contents of the second. From the way it was wrapped, it had to be clothing. If it was something Black had picked out... Belle's insides roiled.

Finding a pair of scissors in the center drawer of the desk, Belle cut the string and unfolded the paper. Nestled within, a diaphanous, white gossamer-fine nightgown, the design of which would make even her girls blush.

Aware it was now or never, Belle undressed and slipped into the gown. It lacked pockets, but had enough ruffles among which she could secrete an essential accessory.

She reached under the settee to retrieve her .41 caliber twin barrel Colt derringer, pausing to ensure both barrels were loaded. Tucking it into the band of the nightgown, she prayed for the courage to do what she was about to do before Black discovered it, or she lost her nerve.

Brushing out her hair with her fingers, she grabbed the bottle of wine, blew the lamp out, and headed upstairs.

Chapter 7

At the top of the staircase, Belle froze at a sound from below. She peeked over the banister and saw a dark shadow ascending the stairs, a glint of something metallic in its grasp.

About to yell a warning, not to protect Black but in self-preservation, her tongue was stayed by a soft, "Hush," in a familiar voice, and she recognized Sara draped in black which concealed everything except the large butcher's knife gripped tightly in her hand.

Sara mouthed, "Just in case."

Black's voice echoed through the dark hallway, "Is that you, my love? Don't make me wait all night."

"C-coming, Uriah," Belle responded as sweetly as possible.

Outside the dimly lit room, she glanced over her shoulder to see Sara a few paces behind, becoming one with the wall.

Inhaling a steadying breath, Belle gathered herself, gave the wooden paneling a gentle push, and stepped into the room, ensuring the door remained ajar.

"I was worried you had decided not to join me," Recumbent on the bed and covered with a thin blanket, Black sounded genuinely concerned.

From where she stood, Belle guessed he was naked… and excited. Plastering a fake smile on her face, she reassured, "I apologize. The beauty of this gown held me enthralled."

She stroked slender fingers over the silky material. "I've never worn something which made me feel so sensuous."

Black laughed, "You shall spend the rest of your life dressed as such for me."

Swallowing the bile rising in her throat this notion engendered, Belle approached the bed. Black reached out to take her hand, tugging her down beside him.

Playing her part, she straddled his strapping frame and curved her lissome body over his to kiss him into dizzy delirium, gyrating against him, hearing him moan in pleasure. A surreptitious peek affirmed he was swept away in the moment, his eyes closed.

Not breaking the kiss, she plucked the derringer from her waistband. In one fluid movement, she straightened up, and shoved the cocked weapon into Black's mouth.

Shocked, he gagged on the cold steel. He tried to speak, but Belle ordered him to, "Shut up. You talk too much. Before I do everyone a favor and rid the world of your hideous face, take a good look at the woman who outwitted you. Was any of this worth Rafe's life?"

Her finger tightened around the trigger. At this distance, the .41 caliber pistol would blow the back of Black's head off. It would cost her a new bed and linen, but she might be able to charge extra for the room where the death of so evil a…

No, Belle. Don't, a voice reverberated around her head. *Justice will not be served this way. You will not reap any reward swinging on the end of a noose.*

Startled, she twisted slightly to gauge whether Sara had experienced a last minute change of heart.

The lack of the expected shot, had indeed prompted the widow to enter the room, slashing her knife wildly, but the caution had not come from her.

Realizing it was her own conscience, Belle faced Black, a split second too late to avoid his fist. He hit her so hard, stars danced before her eyes. The blow catapulted her off the bed, and she tumbled onto the floor, her jaw throbbing.

Sara lunged at her hated enemy, but the blade sank harmlessly into the pillow he held up to protect himself.

Cold rage consuming him — he refused to be bested by two women — Black jerked the pillow sharply, catching Sara off guard, and she tripped, landing in a heap next to Belle.

Through blurry eyes, Belle surmised this was not the first fight he had engaged in to save his sorry hide.

The thud of boots rushing up the stairs drew the attention of all three to the bedroom door. His gun drawn, Sheriff Clinton Baines burst into the room, struggling to make sense of the chaotic scene.

Naked, but determined to regain control of the situation, Black leaped to his feet and jabbed an angry finger at the women, "Baines, arrest these two whores. They just—"

The thunderclap of twin revolvers discharging, exploded behind Baines. The report echoed in the sheriff's ears, as the bullets whooshed past his cheeks to strike Black in the chest, propelling him backwards, his arms flailing as he toppled over the footboard.

Baines whirled around, firing into the darkness, but there was no one to be seen. He raced downstairs to the saloon to search for the murderer.

Hauling themselves upright, the women studied the dead man sprawled on the floor with little sympathy. Sara collected the discarded knife along with Belle's derringer and, while the sheriff was absent, hid them in another room.

Grabbing the bottle, and a robe to protect Belle's modesty, Sara led her friend down to the bar. Hoping to calm their nerves, the two took turns drinking the cheap wine which was half-empty by the time Baines returned.

"Did you find the killer, Sheriff?" Belle's question sounded slightly slurred, the alcohol numbing some of her anxiety.

"No. Was anyone else upstairs besides the three of you?" Baines pinned the pair with a penetrating gaze.

"Not that we were aware," Sara answered for them both.

"And what exactly *were* you all doing up there?" He might not be the sharpest tool in the box, but Baines recognized when something did not ring true.

"Black summoned me to his room to sign over Jeremiah's deed," Sara lied. "I had no idea Belle would be there too."

Baines appraised the other woman who seemed intent on draining the bottle, spotting the tremors in her hand.

"What about you, Belle? Why are you dressed like one of your girls?"

"He wanted the deed to the saloon. I thought I might be able to *charm* him out of that idea. I had barely set foot inside the room when he went berserk. It was an unprovoked attack." She shuddered delicately, and blew a forlorn sigh accompanied by a solitary tear.

"We were scared for our lives, Sheriff," Sara tacked on to validate Belle's story.

"I could be forgiven for suspecting it was a setup for murder. The pair of you had a motive to kill Uriah Black. It's lucky I arrived when I did."

"Why *did* you come, Sheriff Baines?" Belle interjected curiously.

"Darndest thing. I was sound asleep, when I was jolted

awake by the craziest notion that I had to get my butt over here urgently. Hell, I might be one of the Apaches' medicine men." He scratched his head at the absurdity of his words. "Anyway, I'll have the mortician collect the body in the morning."

"Thank you, Sheriff," Belle offered a placatory smile, as Baines nodded a goodbye and strode out of the saloon.

Epilogue

"What will you do now?" Belle asked when Sara took one last gulp of wine and prepared to leave.

"I have no idea. I will probably return to my sister's in Phoenix for now, or I may travel. Who knows."

"You could stay here and help me run the place," Belle offered.

"Nah, I'm worth more than you pay," Sara grinned and, gathering her shawl, bid Belle a pleasant evening and a successful life.

Alone, Belle retrieved the weapons Sara had secreted, replacing the derringer under the settee and the knife to its block in the kitchen.

The pillow she burned in the potbelly stove.

Picking up the lantern from the bar, Belle headed for the staircase, to be halted by two men talking. Their voices appeared to be coming from the Faro table.

Hardly daring to breathe, she pivoted on her heel.

"Ha, you should have seen Baines's face when I whispered in his ear. Thought he was going to jump outta his skin."

"An amusing sight and no mistake, Jerem—"

Belle raised the lantern to illuminate the room. Abruptly, the conversation stopped. With some trepidation, given the events of the evening, she approached the table, keeping a wary eye on the front door of the saloon, just in case.

There was no one there but, in the middle of the table lay a bag, the type of bag used to carry silver ore, and this one contained a large amount.

She murmured a heartfelt thank you to whoever was thoughtful enough to repay their debt before they left.

She also noticed, slung over the Faro dealer's chair, two blue-finished Colt, Single Action, Army pistols in their holsters.

Plucking them from their perch, Belle pledged to protect the weapons and display them on the wall behind her office desk with pride.

Turning to leave, a half-smile curved her lips at the soft chink of glasses touching in a salute, and the faint echo of laughter.

Dipping her head in tacit acknowledgement, Belle climbed the stairs of *her* saloon to her room, shoulders high.

Tomorrow is another day!

The Sacrificial Lamb

Chapter 1

Beside an Unmarked Grave
Outside the Bridgeport Cemetery
During the Waning Crescent Moon

Crystal Rae pointed the thirty-eight caliber Smith and Wesson revolver at the woman's head as she forced the latter to bind her husband's wrists.

"Make sure it's good and tight," Crystal instructed cheerfully. "You've both been a delight tonight. I assure you this will be over soon, and you shall be free to go."

"So, why are we in this cemetery and why, for the love of God are you making me tie Fred up?" The wife's question was garbled by her sobs as she completed her captor's order.

Checking the bonds, Crystal was impressed at the woman's skill with knots. "Very nice," she remarked. "You didn't happen to be a girl scout, did ya?"

Remembering how she met the couple in a bar outside Clarksburg, each step of the carefully rehearsed routine ran through her mind. First ply them with enough alcohol to get them interested in something more. Promises of pot and a hint of a three-way to get them to their car and, finally, her revolver to coax them into the cemetery.

This was her fourth time. Beyond getting the pair drunk, her first attempt was unsuccessful, but the subsequent...

...her thoughts returned to the present.

At no point during the evening had they given any indication they were into rope play... *except that knot... I guess everyone has their secrets*, she concluded.

Shrugging her shoulders, she corrected herself, "Nah. I'm guessin' the two of you are just into kinky shit."

With that, Crystal kicked the woman in the back of her knees, crumpling her to the ground. Curling her fingers through the woman's hair, Crystal dragged her to the opposite side of the unmarked grave.

The wife screamed in excruciating pain, and clawed at Crystal's arm, desperate to break free.

Fred shouted, "Please, don't hurt, Nancy. We'll do whatever you want, just please stop."

Crystal trussed up Nancy in the same manner as Fred, then hoisted her into a kneeling position. The couple faced each other across the low mound.

Pulling a permanent marker from her jean's pocket, Crystal used her teeth to remove the cap, and marked a witch's triple moon tattoo, a crescent on either side of a full moon, on her victims' foreheads.

Swinging the pistol back and forth between the pair she commanded, "If you value your lives, you had best repeat my chant."

Turning, she slithered out of her clothes, revealing the same triple moon motif tattooed across her back. In a graceful sweep, she faced them, flaunting her naked body.

Downing a handful of *magic* mushrooms, she swayed like a willow bending in the wind, chanting, "Oh, Goddess Rhoda Ward, our mother witch, murdered by witless fools..."

Crystal had grown up with the story of Rhoda Ward.

A young woman of the late eighteenth century, charged with being a witch on three seperate occasions, had tricked her accusers *twice* into believing she was innocent when truth be told, she was a Blood Witch attested to by her ability to spit up blood and bent sewing needles. Regrettably, the third time was *not* a charm.

Singularly lacking in any supernatural powers, Crystal remained unwavering in her conviction that she was a direct descendant of Rhoda who, once restored to life, would impart her knowledge on the budding witch.

"...return to those who revere you."

As Crystal's gyrations became frenzied, the half-hearted recitation from her 'offering' pissed her off, and she fired a shot into the night sky.

This motivated the couple into proclaiming their desire for the witch to arise from her slumber, with panicked vigor.

Much better, Crystal ruminated with a sardonic smile.

She continued her bizarre refrain, "Sacred Mother, accept these two sacrifices in your name."

In unison, the pair chorused, "Sacred Mother, accept these two—" then fell silent at the word *sacrifice*.

Nancy gasped, "*Sacrifice?*"

Fred entreated, "Please, n—"

The .38 slug burrowed into Fred's skull, in the center of the full moon, leaving a proverbial crater. His body slumped onto the grave, blood oozing from the wound to soak into the grass.

Before the scream could escape Nancy's throat, Crystal's second shot mimicked her first, dropping the wife on top of her husband.

Her pappy had taught her to shoot well.

Raising the revolver above her head with both hands, she

offered it up to the Waning Crescent Moon of Destruction, shouting, "Arise, Rhoda Ward. Arise."

All she heard was the croaking of toads and chirping of crickets.

Crystal stood in deferential silence. Her eyes, slightly glazed by the mushrooms, scanned the darkness for any movement, registering nothing except the usual hallucinogenic glare around the moon, and twinkling solar system.

Disappointed, Crystal slumped onto the grass. A shiver raced up her back, pebbling her flesh.

Looking at the two sacrificial lambs, she sighed, "I guess they were not pure enough."

Hefting them off Rhoda's unmarked grave, Crystal stretched out on it, watching the 'shroom-induced shooting stars whiz across space.

Confident of her kinship with the long-departed witch, she entreated, "Rho, Rho, I wish you'd tell me what kinda offering you're after. It's not that I object to killing them, it's more having to pick them up in bars."

As the night wore on and the cold began to take its toll on her naked body, Crystal readied herself to address the final chore of the evening.

Shrugging into her tank top and jeans, she grabbed Nancy, the lighter of the two, by the feet and hauled her through the gates of the cemetery, to the once elaborate mausoleum at the far side.

The crumbling vault housed not only several stone sarcophagi and one dilapidated wooden casket but also, of late, a heap of corpses from Crystal's previous kills, along with several bags of quicklime to minimize the stench of decomposition.

Since Crystal was a little girl, her mother had drummed into her the need to tidy up after oneself. "See, Mama, I'm not leaving my damned toys all over the floor," Crystal yelled at the exposed skeleton in the broken coffin, wishing it was her detested mother, not a long forgotten member of a local family who believed they were worthy of memorializing. "They're all stacked neatly in the corner."

She heaved Nancy onto the pile, covered her with the lime, then returned for Fred. As expected, moving him was a struggle and, not for the first time, she wished Rhoda's grave was closer.

Breathing heavily, she leaned against the doorframe to collect herself.

"Jesus, if I'm gonna keep this up, I better get in shape," she huffed, before dragging Fred inside and dousing him with lime.

Exiting the vault, she secured the door tightly, and snapped shut the vintage padlock she had bought to replace the original.

Only one who needs to get in is me.

Finished, she retraced her steps to the couple's 1959 Pontiac Bonneville two door hardtop and set off to her home atop Wolf Summit on the other side of Clarksburg.

Chapter 2

The drive home was anything but soothing. Her failure to summon Rhoda Ward in the cemetery had left a bad taste in her mouth, and now she had to ditch the shiny white boat of a car with the sun breaking the horizon.

At least she had possessed the foresight to catch a cab to the bar, instead of driving her beat up Plymouth.

As she cleared Clarksburg, and headed towards the Summit, Crystal spotted a solitary figure standing on the opposite verge, looking as though he was trying to thumb a lift.

At this early hour, the other motorists ignored the hitch-hiker but not Crystal. Doing a U-turn, she eased the Pontiac to a stop alongside the stranger, and flicked the button to roll down the passenger side power window.

Crystal, who had never owned a car with fancy accessories, was fascinated by this mechanism but kept her composure to conceal the fact, the car was not hers. She did, however, slide one hand under the driver seat, to retrieve the buck knife she had stashed there.

Secreting the knife under her right thigh, she contemplated her next move.

Rho, I apologize for my pitiful tribute. Given ignorant men murdered you because they feared you, perhaps a single male is a commensurate offering — she had no clue whether the phrase was correct, but she had heard it on TV and thought it was something smart people might say — *to resurrect you.*

Looking the man up and down, she smiled and with her best Appalachian charm cooed, "Hey there, cutie, where ya headin'?"

A return grin spread across the hitchhiker's scruffy face.

Crystal could not describe what was on his chin as a bona fide beard, nor the fuzz clinging to his upper lip as a moustache, *but this was West Virginia. If a beard wasn't long enough to kiss the second button on a flannel shirt, it was just stubble,* she reflected internally.

"Heading into Clarksburg and hopefully a decent breakfast," he replied in a crisp Midwestern accent. "Though, I'm not sure what the town has to offer."

"Hop in. I'm happy to take you back into town."

"Weren't you going the other way? I couldn't possibly inconvenience you."

"Shug, what kinda Christian would I be if I left ya stranded 'long side the road. I'll take ya to the best diner in town." Crystal beamed.

"If you're sure it's not an imposition."

Crystal lied without batting an eyelid, "None at all. Looks like it's your lucky day. Truth be told, I forgot I needed to pick up some stuff at the market before I head home."

The man opened the car door and climbed in. Tossing his pack in the back seat, he noticed a man's jacket and a white, knitted sweater, the latter of which he found odd, because it did not fit his chauffeur's apparent style. He decided not to ask. They probably belonged to her folks, and it was not his business anyway.

Nevertheless, as he clipped on his seat belt, he glanced at her ring finger for the tell-tale signs she was married or engaged. Apparently not.

Presuming she was borrowing her parent's car, he settled into the seat as the whale of a Pontiac purred back to Clarksburg.

Crystal blared John Denver's *Country Roads* on the Bonneville's radio, so loudly, the speakers' paper cones crackled and threatened to tear from their frames.

Her window down, despite the morning chill, Crystal's dirty blonde hair billowed along the edge of the door and whipped about her face as she shared her rendition of the song with the countryside.

In vain, the hitchhiker tried to start a conversation until, certain his eyes were about to rupture, he turned the music down.

"Hey," Crystal objected. "Why'd ya do that? I was enjoying it."

"Lord, girl, I thought I was going to go deaf. Besides, I've been trying to talk to you."

"Well, whatcha wanna talk about?" she countered, piqued that he had cut her concert short.

"How about something easy, like your name?" her passenger suggested brightly. "I'm Colton."

Crystal studied him, trying to decide whether he was telling her the truth. She had heard the name used in a Western. Frowning, she asked, "Are you a…"

Her eyes on the stranger, she did not realize the Pontiac was drifting into oncoming traffic. The blare of a tractor trailer's horn snapped her attention back to the road.

To correct the trajectory, Crystal oversteered, and the large car fishtailed, careening toward the ditch.

She yanked the steering wheel in the opposite direction making the tires on the Bonneville squeal in protest. Slamming on the brakes, dirt spraying up from the shoulder, Crystal controlled the vehicle and brought it to a stop.

Ramming the shifter car into park, Crystal howled with laughter. "Yeehaw. I should be a stunt driver."

Colton, on the other hand, failed to see the amusement in her antics. "What the fuck are you doing? Are you trying to kill us, you lunatic?"

Crystal reached for the knife tucked under her leg, but thought better of brandishing it, making do with, "Nobody calls me crazy. Ever. Don't you dare say that to me again."

"I'm sorry," Colton placated. "But how about easing up on the gas so we can make it to breakfast."

The two remained silent as they passed through Clarksburg and continued along Route 50 to Bridgeport.

At the sign stating Bridgeport was five miles away, Colton ventured, "I thought we were stopping in Clarksburg."

"No, I told you I was taking you to the best breakfast in town."

***

Satellite Cafe
Bridgeport

Relieved they had arrived without further incident, Colton alighted and rounded the car to the driver's door.

Watching him through the rearview mirror, Crystal took the opportunity to return the buck knife to its hiding place under the seat, her fingers grazing against the .38 tucked neatly alongside. The knowledge it still held four cartridges elicited a surge of power and control.

She looked up, seeing Colton through her window, reaching for the door handle.

In a gentlemanly fashion, ingrained by his upper-middle class Chicago background, he opened the door for Crystal, repeating the gesture at the cafe's entrance.

Crystal brushed this off as the hitchhiker's attempt to impress her out of her jeans.

The pair chose a booth at the back, sat down, and perused the menu. A good-natured waitress, dressed in pink and white, approached their table.

The uniform's faded colors implied the woman had worked at the cafe for several years, the snug fit suggesting that she had no problem sampling the food.

Cracking on a piece of gum as she spoke, the waitress asked Colton, "What do you and your girl want?"

Before Crystal could rebut this assumption, Colton, in the role of the Alpha male, ordered, "We'll have two of your breakfast house specials. Does it come with grits?" He had never eaten grits before, but understood it was something every Southerner was supposed to live on, so he figured they were worth a try.

"Sure thing, shugs," the waitress affirmed without writing it down. "Y'all want some bacon with that?"

"Definitely." Colton nodded. "Coffee, and a couple of slices of white toast. None of that crappy wholewheat stuff. Oh, and make sure the eggs are over medium. My girl here hates 'em soft."

"Well, actually—" Crystal, who much preferred runny yolks, tried to cut in but missed the opportunity, the waitress was already heading back to the kitchen.

Irritated with Colton's arrogance, she kicked him in the shin.

"Ouch," he grumbled. "Why did you do that?"

"Cuz, I don't like people ordering for me. 'Specially since now I have to eat hard eggs and can't dip my toast."

Chapter 3

The pair chatted while they ate. They discussed the weather, and how much they were against the Vietnam War and President Nixon.

Talk of their respective families covered the bare minimum until Colton said, "Yeah, my ol' man still lives in Chicago."

"What about your mama?" Crystal inquired delicately.

Colton fell silent, stabbing his eggs with his fork. "She died when I was about twelve. My dad said it was an accident, some bullshit about her falling down the stairs, but I never believed him."

"What do you think happened?"

"I think he got drunk and beat her to death," the fury in Colton's voice was not lost on Crystal.

Despite this, the notion of an unsolved murder intrigued her. "Why do you think that? Did you see the body?"

"Hardly," Colton huffed. "I was just a kid. He's not crazy enough to show me his handiwork. Besides, he's a detective with the CPD. Nobody would believe me."

His appetite gone, Colton played with his food, saying,

without lifting his eyes from the plate, "If that ain't a kick in the behind, I tried to join the force to prove he was guilty and have him fried in the electric chair."

He took a drink of his water. A laugh escaped him into the bottom of the glass, "'Cept, for some reason, I failed the psych eval. Something about unresolved anger issues. Isn't that a hoot?" He slammed the glass down, shattering it in his hand. A jagged edge sliced his palm.

Hearing the shards hit the floor, the waitress appeared like Rosie the Robot from the *Jetsons*, broom and dustpan in hand. Before sweeping up the mess, she grasped Colton's wrist.

With the expertise of a mother examining her careless child's wound, she tsked, "You're lucky the glass didn't cut any deeper, otherwise I'd be sending you to the ER. You'd best get yourself to the men's room and wash that out. Then come over to the counter and I'll bandage it."

Colton was about to tell her to mind her own business when her brow furrowed, and she said, "Now, young man."

Realizing it was unlikely he had encountered an Appalachian mother, Crystal fought to suppress a giggle which did not go unnoticed by the older woman.

"As for you, young lady, I don't know what you said to the poor boy to set him off like that, but you'd be wise to curb that tongue of yours."

Glaring at the waitress who had turned to sweep up the mess, Crystal made a mental note to return to the diner and sacrifice the bitch... *just because.*

When Colton reappeared from the men's room, a bloodied paper towel wrapped around his hand, Crystal was amused to see he did as instructed, meeting the waitress, who had the first-aid kit out already, at the counter.

The waitress turned his hand palm up to check for any

stray slivers. Taking a bottle of mercurochrome from the box, she unscrewed the cap and brushed it on the cut.

Colton yelped in pain.

What a baby, Crystal thought. *I'd be doing him a favor to take him out of this life... but how?*

She was still contemplating how to coax her breakfast companion to Rhoda Ward's grave, when Colton returned to the table, but did not sit down.

"Look, I appreciate the ride and breakfast, but I think it's time for me to push on."

Crystal's lips flattened at the thought of losing her prospective sacrifice.

"Please, Colton, have a seat and finish your breakfast. After all, it's on me and I would hate for you to was—"

"No," Colton interrupted. "In good faith, I cannot allow you to pay for my breakfast. My wallet is in my backpack. I'll just run out to the car, get it, and pay for the meal."

Before Crystal could say a word, Colton was at the door, and heading to the car.

"Fuck," she growled to herself. "If I'm gonna do something I better do it now."

Opening her purse, she dug for the vial of yellow pills she had stolen from her mother's dresser drawer. Trying to read the label brought her lack of education into sharp focus as she struggled to pronounce the word Diazepam, better known as Valium, skipping over it to the dosage: *5 mg three times a day.*

If these beauties made her mama manageable, a handful should leave Colton as compliant as a lamb.

She tipped several onto the table then, using her glass, crushed the pills. Sweeping the ground medication into her hand, she brushed it into Colton's coffee cup, refilled and stirred it, then slid it over to his side as he went to the counter to settle the bill.

Returning to the booth, Colton smiled. "Thank you for the ride and the company. I hope we can meet again sometime." He slung his backpack over his shoulder, and prepared to leave, but Crystal wheedled.

"How about one last cup of coffee before you go? It's still a little chilly out, it'll warm you up."

He glanced at the door, and then at her beautiful, pleading eyes, "Fine, just one."

Colton resumed his seat, lifted the cup, toasted her, and drained the contents. Odd chunks of some unidentifiable substance trickled down his throat, nearly choking him.

He assumed it was coffee grounds, given it was a cheap blend, but there was something about the bits which didn't feel right, they were too… coarse. He spat out one. It was a fragment of a coffee-stained yellow pill.

Precious second ticked by while he stared at the offending granule, waiting for his brain to catch up to his eyes.

Valium. The word teased his mind. *That's a similar yellow.*

He had learned about the drug at the police academy, before he was booted.

Surely, she had not…

Trying to convince himself otherwise, Colton growled, "What the fuck have you done?" Keenly aware, given the method of delivery, that the opiate was already being absorbed into his bloodstream.

Crystal's mouth moved as she spouted some doubtless nonsensical reasoning, but he could not decipher what she was saying, and his vision had blurred. The dose had triggered Central Nervous System Depression, surprising them both by the speed with which it took effect.

Colton swiped at her, but missed, stumbling over the chair and overturning the table, spilling food everywhere.

As if by magic, the waitress materialized at their booth,

even less grateful to be serving this couple. Seeing Colton trying to scramble upright, she gritted her teeth. "Now what's wrong?"

Playing a part of the concerned girlfriend, Crystal complete with crocodile tears wept, "I-I don't know. P-please help me get him to the car so I can take him to hospital."

Sighing, the waitress called, "Billy, grab Mack and help this boy out to their car."

Two burly men, with the combined IQ of a rock, appeared from the kitchen and strong-armed Colton to the Bonneville.

Colton tried to wriggle out of their grip, but the stupor induced by the Valium left him helpless. His pleas not to put him into the car sounded like incoherent babble.

Carelessly, the heavies tossed him, face-first, onto the back seat, on top of the white sweater. Colton's last conscious thought before everything went dark was, *the perfume on this is not Crystal's.*

Chapter 4

Colton's eyes fluttered open, which did not help. He was engulfed in darkness, save the smallest ray of light bleeding in from what he guessed might to be an entrance to his prison. He tried to move his hands to register they were bound behind him, and his legs were shackled.

He kicked out, discovering, too late, that this was a bad idea. His feet met something pliable, which tumbled onto his legs and raised a cloud of something he could not distinguish in the process.

He choked on the dust, his hacking cough echoing in the dark confines. Struggling for a breath, and to free his legs from whatever pinned them down, a fetid odor taunted his nostrils, familiar yet unwelcome. Putting two and two together, he guessed the cloud was probably quicklime, and he was in somebody's death pit.

That somebody could only be Crystal!

In a rage, he yelled, "Crystal, get your crazy ass in here and release me. *Now.*"

There was no reply.

Gradually, Colton's vision adapted to the gloom. He made

out the shape of the broken casket as well as the stack of bodies by the wall in the corner.

His nose and lungs burned from the toxic dust, but it was the stench of rotting flesh which he found overwhelming. Ignoring it, as best he could, Colton decided to see whether he could find anything sharp enough to cut his bonds.

Scooting around on his butt, Colton shuffled across to the coffin. Slowly, relying on the miraculously intact base for leverage, he managed to inch upright.

His fingers explored the edge of the casket's rotten, ragged wood, collecting splinters along the way. In a mixed blessing, one finger caught against a sharp hunk of metal, he presumed was an old, spiked nail, originally used to fasten the lid down.

Colton felt blood ooze from the wound. "Great, I'll probably get tetanus, on top of being murdered."

In earnest, he rubbed the rope against the aged metal. Every now and then, he misjudged the distance and nicked his skin.

The movement of the thin beam of light across the floor, informed him of the sun's trek across the sky. It was nearing sunset when tugging at the strands he registered, despite his best efforts, he was only about halfway through the rope.

Colton knew Crystal would return to finish whatever insanity she had in mind.

For the first time in his life, abject fear gnawed at him. He had grown numb to the rage that dwelled within him, but to recognize the single emotion which he had seen in the eyes of others at their end was... almost... liberating?

Why does this make me feel more alive? he pondered this briefly, then stopped wasting time, and returned to the matter at hand, informing the skeleton, whose casket he was desecrating further, that, "I am not going down without a fight."

The pinprick of light vanished from the door frame, casting the mausoleum into complete darkness. At the crunch of footsteps, Colton froze. He heard keys jangle and the clunk of a padlock clicking open.

Hopping to the wall next to the door, he held his breath as the door creaked open.

A beam from a flashlight swept back and forth around the house of the dead, settling on the disheveled pile of bodies.

The dark shape of a .38 police pistol accompanied the flashlight. It was being held in the person's right hand away from the torch.

A maneuver taught at the police academy, when officers had to carry both, because most shooters would aim at the light, missing the patrolman's vitals. He had no idea how Crystal knew this, but he was not about to ask.

In a singsong voice, Crystal trilled, "Colton, come out, come out, wherever you are. I know you're still here, cutie."

As the light swung in his direction, a surge of adrenaline gripped him. Jerking his wrists hard against the rope, the last few strands snapped. His feet still bound, he lunged forward, knocking Crystal off her feet.

She fired the pistol blindly; the flare from the barrel illuminated the shock painting her face. Torch and gun skittered out of her grip when she landed on her back with Colton's bulk on top of her.

Kicking and howling like an alley cat, Crystal fought back.

Grabbing her hair, Colton slammed her skull against the stone floor, momentarily stunning her. A dark stream trickled out from under her head.

Colton found the buck knife sheathed to Crystal's belt.

Pulling it out, he considered slitting her throat, but wanted to free his feet first.

Plunging the razor-sharp blade into the rope, Colton sliced his bonds. He heard Crystal moaning, and saw her stir. He had to hurry.

With the last bite of the knife, the rope fell away. The rush of blood to his extremities felt like the sting of a thousand fiery needles, making him stagger.

Instead of trying to battle Crystal, Colton deemed it wiser to take the knife and flee.

Pain shot through his legs as he ran through the dimly lit cemetery, hoping he was heading for Crystal's car.

Behind him, Colton heard the click of a pistol's hammer. He dodged to the right as the weapon clapped its deadly thunder, and a projectile whizzed past him, clipping the top of a tombstone knocking its cherub to the ground.

Ducking behind a larger headstone, Colton listened intently for the stealthy whisper of footsteps. He was at a distinct disadvantage. He had no clue how many bullets she had left in her pistol, and… more importantly…

…this was Crystal's hunting ground and he did not doubt she was an expert when it came to tracking her prey.

That said, he possessed skills she could not fathom.

The soft hiss of grass being crushed underfoot caught his attention. He strained to hear from where it originated, because it was not the same direction as the shot.

Staying low, he crept backwards, pausing every so often by another tombstone. The cackle of Crystal's maniacal laughter dared him to take an occasional peek.

The first time he risked this, she pulled the trigger, and the bullet grazed his ear. The next time, she taunted, "Here, turkey, turkey, gobble, gobble, gobble."

Colton threw a rock to his right, drawing her fire in that direction, as he ran left.

Two more shots chased him, one burrowing into a nearby tree trunk.

The other clipped his leg, which toppled him onto the soft earth. With a neat duck and roll, he vaulted upright. Hobbling at a fair pace, he burst through the gates of the cemetery aiming for the set of headlights shining like a homing beacon less than twenty yards away.

Crystal followed, "Run, run as fast as you can, I'll catch you, Gingerbread man."

Looking over his shoulder, he spotted her closing in on him, dark blood oozing from the cut on her head.

She misquoted a line from the movie *The Night of the Living Dead*, "Run, Barbara, they're coming to get you."

Tired of Crystal's crap, Colton turned to face her, brandishing her knife in defense. The phrase, *Don't bring a knife to a gunfight,* mocked him.

"Come on, bitch, bring it on," he yelled, wincing as she pulled the trigger expecting a bullet to hit him in the chest. A second dull click told him the gun was empty.

Undeterred, Crystal raced headlong at Colton, firing the empty revolver as though bullets would appear magically.

Trying to ward her off, Colton lashed out with the buck knife.

Ducking under the blade, Crystal bowled Colton off his feet. As the pair tumbled onto the damp grass, the knife fell from his grasp.

Crystal straddled Colton's chest, pummeling him with the butt of the gun. A wave of anger prevented him from submitting.

Regaining his composure, he threw a solid jab to her jaw, sending the banshee off him and onto her stomach. Before she could gather herself, Colton jumped on her back.

Spying several planks which had created a crude boxing ring, Colton pounded her forehead against the wood.

Bellowing in pain, Crystal refused to concede. "Goddess Rhoda, give me the strength to kill this bastard."

"You want a death tonight, bitch?" Colton growled in her ear. "Try this on for size." Seeing the knife on the ground, glittering under the crescent moon, he grabbed the hilt.

Before Crystal could reply, Colton yanked up her head by her hair, and drew the blade across her throat from ear to ear. Blood spurted across the grass.

As she gasped for breath, gagging on her blood, he added one last indignity.

Forcing Crystal's mouth open, Colton sliced off her tongue with her own blade.

As her life force drained from her eyes, he chuckled. "This will make a fine addition to my collection, as well as saving my ears from your shrewish voice."

He tucked the trophy into his pocket and turned to leave.

The ground surrounding the rectangle rumbled. Colton presumed it was an earthquake, but the feminine tone speaking from somewhere behind him suggested something different.

"Oh, dear girl, you finally discovered the key to my resurrection. *Your* blood, my distant offspring, was the missing ingredient required to awaken me."

Colton spun around to see the specter of a nude woman, her neck at a curious angle as though the victim of a hanging.

Her eyes blazed fiery red as she returned Colton's gaping stare.

"As for you boy." The spirit held up her palm to Colton, holding him motionless. "You shall be taking my place in Hell."

Frozen, he watched the wraith meld with Crystal. The erstwhile serial killer rose to her feet, brushed herself off and, running her hands over her figure, healed the wounds peppering her new body.

Picking up the knife, she twirled it in her fingers, and before he could so much as blink, thrust it into his throat.

Colton collapsed onto his grassy grave. Boney fingers and hands skewered out of the dirt to claw at his body, wresting him into the Stygian depths below.

Before he vanished for eternity, the witch plucked Crystal's tongue from his pocket. Slipping it into her mouth, she crooned, "I hope you meet your victims, you bastard, and they are given the pleasure of reciprocating the torment you inflicted."

***

Rhoda stretched her arms toward the moon, eyes closing as every thought and memory held by Crystal merged into her mind until the transformation was complete.

Glancing at the headlights of the Bonneville, she chuckled quietly. "Before we begin our new life of mischief and debauchery, I believe we ought to visit your mama, girl, to seek a little retribution for the wickedness that reprehensible descendant of mine wrought on you."

SQUATTERS' RIGHTS

Chapter 1

July 2, 1813

Hannson's Reach was a speck of land located just within the American territorial waters off the coast of northern Maine. It fell under US dominion during the War of 1812, when a contingent of American soldiers was sent to the island to clear it of a Canadian brigade assigned there by the British Crown.

The Americans infiltrated the island under the cover of darkness, to discover the enemy had abandoned their base. Curiously, ships flying the Union Jack remained moored to the Reach's sole harbor, ready to set sail at a moment's notice.

Further investigation of the makeshift barracks nestled in the heart of the island revealed they were stocked with supplies and, oddly enough, the inhabitants' personal items.

The tables in the dining tent were laden with meals, waiting for the soldiers to sit down and feast.

Fear gripped the invaders, who refused to partake of the still warm food for fear it was a poisoned trap.

The only remnant of a military presence was a 5.5-inch light howitzer, which appeared to have been used in the defense of the outpost. Pointing skywards, it had fired a ridiculous number of projectiles, attested to by the casings surrounding the weapon.

The new arrivals removed any trace of their predecessors from the land, stripped the base and reduced everything the former occupants had left, including the ships, to ash. Anything not combustible was dumped into the Atlantic.

Once the island was cleared, the Americans established a forward post, to defend the fledgling country against future incursions from the British, or any other foreign power.

July 2, 2013

The residents of Hannson's Reach were immersed in their final preparations for the island's bicentennial.

Signs and banners celebrating the bravery of the American soldiers who, under the blistering barrage of cannon and howitzer fire, liberated the island from the clutches of the barbarous Canadians, driving them into the ocean. The descendants of those same brave souls constituted the citizenry of the Reach.

Throughout the centuries, the population had hovered at or around five hundred. An important statistic because this meant not only were the island's resources dispersed evenly but also, it was the minimum number required to ensure the inhabitants could retain evolutionary potential in perpetuity.

While there was no official policy enforcing this population level, it was universally, if tacitly, accepted as though guided by unseen forces.

"Mayor Cheatham," a rosy-cheeked woman addressed a tall, smartly-dressed gentleman.

"Ah, Edwina," the Mayor, Wilbur Cheatham, replied affably. "What can I do for you?"

"I wanted to let you know, the children are all set to reenact the invasion. They look so cute in their military uniforms. I think the sewing guild outdid themselves this year."

"I cannot wait." The mayor gave her a broad grin.

"Unfortunately, none of the children wanted to play the Canadians so, we had to use the cutouts again for them to storm and, I must say, the errr… enemy… look the worse for wear. Might I suggest we replace them before the next observance?"

"I will take note of the request, Edwina, and bring it up with the town council at our next meeting. If you could give me some idea of the replacement cost, it would help."

Edwina flipped through her usual over-stuffed folder, its worn cover adorned with garish paisley flowers, and handed a page complete with itemized costs to the mayor with a wry smile. "Well, your honor, I just so happen—"

"I had no doubt." He chuckled as he scanned the list. He did not have the heart to tell Edwina, the island's coffers were not deep enough to cover her extravagant requests, especially the automatronic figures.

The fishing grounds beyond the breakwaters had fallen victim to corporate over-harvesting, caused by their humongous ships and nets. The local watermen stood little chance against them.

Edwina closed the binder, securing it with a large rubber band. Ignoring the mayor's amusement at her zeal, she noted, "It's a shame your wife and her partners are not here today for the celebration."

"True, but they needed to go to Augusta to renew their realtor licenses."

She sighed, "Well, business always comes first. They were fortunate the ferry happened to be in port bringing the last of the supplies for the bicentennial."

Hannson's Reach was so small, the only agencies aware of it were the Coast Guard, the ferry master whose service to and from the island occurred when summoned rather than a regular schedule, and, of course, the Internal Revenue Service — taxes were inescapable, no matter the size of the catch.

As the last of the sun's rays flashed their brilliant green from the horizon, the festivities on the island were launched in all their splendor.

A flotilla of decorated fishing boats, illuminated with Christmas lights, sailed past the beach, horns blaring noisily.

A single boat belonging to the harbormaster beached on the shore, allowing children, in full military regalia, to disembark, whooping and hollering, as they overran the imitation enemy, claiming victory over the island not only for the United States, but also for the future residents of Hannson's Reach.

Then, the entirety of the population settled down to enjoy an astonishing display of colorful fireworks.

As the first projectile burst in a dazzling blue shower over the island, a blinding azure flash responded in kind, dwarfing the pyrotechnics.

None of the residents stood a chance of escaping its brilliance. Music continued to blare through the various speakers, but there was no one to enjoy it.

In an instant, not a soul remained on Hannson's Reach.

Standing in the hold of his craft, Druote, commander of the Decronian commercial ship, *DSS Ravager*, watched as the last of the Earthlings were conveyed to the suspended animation pods.

As the ship's crew prepared for their intergalactic trip to their home planet, Druote grumbled to his second in command, "We have returned to this rock repeatedly over the last 100,000 years of these creatures' time, and I have yet to understand the fascination the elites on our planet have for these meat sacks. Not only are they hideous to look at, but they stink."

The Decronians were silicon-based life forms, standing more than ten feet tall. Their chromium clothing indistinguishable from their flesh.

His subordinate huffed, "Some find them appetizing, a delicacy, I guess. Most just keep them as pets. It is supposed to be a sign of power and wealth."

"Whatever," the commander scoffed. "Prepare for the wormhole jump. The sooner I can get these maggots off my vessel the better."

The ship shot vertically into low earth orbit, reaching speeds of 3,600 miles per hour, before coming to an instant halt. A hole seemed to tear into the fabric of space before swallowing the ship whole.

The entire event was tracked by the IRS from their black ops facility concealed beneath the old Loring Air Force Base — after all, taxes must be paid.

Chapter 2

S pecial Agent Joaquin Navarro was sitting at his desk
sorting through the stack of reports generated during
the previous night. One troubled him. A case which had
developed in Hannson's Reach. Tossing it to the side, he
pressed his intercom.

"Yes, Agent Navarro?"

Joaquin hated conversing with his Administrative
Assistant, but Ophelia Dulles had been with the service
longer than anyone could remember. Some speculated she
predated the IRS, and was actually one of the first eight
female clerks hired in 1862 by its predecessor, the Bureau of
Internal Revenue.

She was also *the* most connected person in the Service—
both domestic and *foreign*.

The woman was extremely old school, which Joaquin
respected and always ensured he addressed her with defer-
ence. "Miss Dulles, is there any word of survivors from the
Hannson incident?"

"On the island no, sir. There is, however, a manifesto

from the *SS Caroline* stating it returned with three passengers bound for Augusta."

"Shit," he muttered under his breath.

"What was that?" Ophelia had the hearing of a bat.

"I, uh, spilled coffee on myself,"

"Mm hmm," she said skeptically.

"Anyway, have you sent agents to collect them?"

"Yes, sir. They arrived in Augusta in time to prevent their scheduled meeting."

"Has the island been buttoned?"

This time, Ophelia muttered something Joaquin could not catch, then said, not bothering to mask her sarcasm, "Yes, sir. This is not my first rodeo."

Truth be told, this was the 4,532nd occasion since the founding of America that the government was forced to cover up a mass abduction.

Before the beginning of the twentieth century it was a much easier task, chalking the sudden demise of a town or a region to the depletion of gold, silver, or whatever other metal men had risked their lives and fortunes to find.

With the advent of the IRS and the spread of modern media, more creative stories had to be invented. Nuclear radiation, foul water, and the like were incorporated.

"If anyone bothers to call, the story is set. Medical waste seemed fitting. Now can we contend with a more important matter, sir?" Ophelia reassured.

He knew what she was about to dredge up.

"Go ahead."

"Yet again the Decronians took off without paying proper export taxes on their cargo. That makes five incursions when they have neglected to settle their bill. Should I file the appropriate paperwork with DC?"

"What and end up wasting years in the Interplanetary Tax Court? No thank you. Just contact the Federation Revenuers and submit a complaint with them directly. It's about time they got off their collective butts and did their jobs. Their ten percent cut doesn't even bother me."

"Yes, sir," Ophelia acknowledged. "Be prepared for Washington to call and chew you out for daring to spend an extra dime."

"What else is new?" was his laconic response as he disconnected.

This was not the job he had signed up for when he joined the IRS. He wanted to arrest mobsters who refused to pay their share of their ill-gotten booty.

But no.

He was in charge of Interplanetary Revenue Investigation, working alongside beings who saw Earth as their playground. Appointing themselves galactic diplomats, they enjoyed flaunting their legal immunity to any law they saw fit.

The three women who had traveled to the state capital to renew their realtors' licenses found themselves escorted to who the hell knew where, by nondescript armed guards.

Questions to their captors — whose eyes were hidden behind black, what had to be government issue, sunglasses — about what the hell was going on and why they had been detained, were met with blank expressions and buttoned lips.

One of the men did condescend to inform the women they could expect a visit within a week to explain everything.

The problem was the visit never materialized.

Until one day a well-dressed man arrived, flashed his IRS credentials, and introduced himself, "Good afternoon, ladies. I am special agent Joaquin Navarro."

"What's so good about it, Agent Navarro?" Agnes

Cheatham shot back. "We have been treated like terrorists. Could you at least tell me the date, and if we are being held in Guantanamo Bay?"

Joaquin chuckled. "I can assure you, my dear Mrs. Cheatham, you are nowhere as dire. In fact, you are housed safely in Maine."

"And why, might I ask, are we being *housed*?" Rochelle Johnson, the oldest of the three women, sniped.

Joaquin placed a manila folder on the table between them, opened it and spread out pictures of dead fish and all manner of toxic waste riddling the island's pristine shores. The ominous tone of his voice hid a darker truth.

"I could give you the standard government BS about your beautiful island being cordoned off owing to serious levels of contamination, but I would be at a loss to tell you where your people went—"

"Our people?" the third member of their partnership, Deloris Summers interjected.

Joaquin ignored the interruption. "More importantly, I need your help to conserve a centuries' old secret."

Looking at Deloris, he admitted, "Yes, ma'am, your families, in fact, the entire population of Hansson's Reach have gone."

"Gone?" the women cried in unison.

Agnes added, "You mean as in dead?"

Joaquin pursed his lips as he searched for the correct words. "Not dead, exactly, but definitely not coming back."

"I have no clue what lunacy you're spewing," Rochelle countered, "but you'd better be more forthcoming with the truth."

Chewing on his lip, he revealed, "Your town, in fact the entire population of the island, was abducted by galactic species collectors. Consider them zoo hunters."

"Zoo hunters?" Deloris screeched.

"They've been doing this since the dawn of man."

"And in all this time no one has tried to stop them?" Deloris sobbed her reproach, devastated to hear the fate of her husband and children.

"I wish we could," Joaquin replied, "but we have neither the technology nor the firepower. To make matters worse," the IRS agent let slip, as he studied the faked pictures, "these gangsters owe the US government trillions in back taxes."

"Ex*cuse* me?" Agnes broke in.

The agent knew it was too late to retract the statement. He was already in for a penny, so might as well throw in the pound.

"Where do you think America gets its bottomless purse? Taxes from its citizens? From businesses? Hardly. We belong to an intergalactic revenue alliance which relies on trade tariffs applied to commerce amongst the different worlds."

The women stared at him as though he were babbling gibberish… because to them he was.

Joaquin did not bother to outline what awaited their friends and family once they reached Decronia. It was too appalling, making do with a flippant, "What's done is done. Now, what I need from you three is to repopulate the island."

"Repopulate?" Agnes repeated her voice rising in disbelief. "In case you hadn't noticed, we are females, meaning it's impossible for us to impregnate one another."

"Good Lord," Joaquin snorted. "That is not what I'm suggesting. I want you to sell the empty properties to prospective buyers. You will each, of course, receive a handsome commission for your efforts."

"What about you? What do you receive?" Delores interjected with no small hint of derision.

"Reimbursement of the cost to clean the island and prepare the houses and shops for sale."

"When will that be?" Agnes chimed in.

"About three years. Until then, you will be under the care of the IRS. If you come up with the bright idea to spill the beans to the media, understand the full weight of the US government will come crashing down on you to make you look as crazy as this story sounds."

As the three shared concerned looks amongst themselves, Joaquin rose and gathered his documents, leaving them with a sunny, "Until we meet again, consider this an extended holiday on the government's dime."

———

Chapter 3

March 23, 2016

For the past three years, the women had languished in the facility which was akin to the famous minimum-security prison often referred to by its inmates as *Club Fed*, minus their prison's satellite television access and *any* conjugal visits.

Instead, in addition to using the gym, pool, and track, they busied themselves with directing the rehabilitation of the island's properties, including the removal and disposal of the former owners' personal items.

The realtors were instrumental in helping the government to choose colors and furnishings aimed at attracting the more discerning buyer.

Their goal was to transform the sleepy fishing island into a new Martha's Vineyard, convincing themselves that the tragedy of the past should not consume their future.

When the first of the nouveau riche, a trending Hollywood couple looking to escape their *dreaded* fame, arrived on the island via the shiny new ferry, with its equally shiny new captain, accompanied by a boatload of paparazzi, word spread quickly among the Gen Zs that Hannson's Reach was *the* place to be.

It did not hurt that the federal government had supplied the island with a state-of-the-art, military grade satellite-based internet.

Finally, the troubles which had faced the three relators were far behind them.

The same could not be said elsewhere in the universe.

At the Edge of the Milky Way

The *Ravager* prepared to exit the wormhole, her crew excited to return to their homes. Extended space travel took its toll no matter the species.

When Druote gave the order to drop the ship into Decronia's orbit, the navigator stared at his commander in horror. "I-I cannot, Commander," he stammered.

"What? Have you lost your mind, Quixous?" The commander accused angrily. "Should I have you relieved?"

Druote stomped across the bridge to the navigation station, grousing, "By the gods, do I have to pilot this entire ship myself?"

Hurriedly, the navigator tried to explain, "No, sir, you do not understand. Decronia is not there." His words preceded the ship's descent into lower orbit.

Where their glittering planet, a thriving civilization, ought to be holding sway over its solar system, filling friends and foe alike with envy at their technological prowess and might, was a dark void liberally besprinkled with immense hunks of cosmic flotsam and jetsam.

Druote barked, "All Stop," and the Ravager came to a jarring halt before it could collide with any of the debris.

Addressing his second, Druote said, "Terian, scan for signs of life."

"Already on it, sir, and we have company off the port side."

The Federation Revenue Destroyer, *FRS Unsympathetic Collectors*, idled behind an enormous chunk of the former planet of Decronia, awaiting its unsuspecting prey.

As with Revenuers anywhere in the galaxy, regardless of the species, excessive force was the rule rather than the exception.

In this case, the collateral damage was beyond excessive.

The destruction of Decronia resulted in its double moons losing their gravitational center, sending them spinning wildly into the solar system's orange dwarf star. Along the way, the larger of the twins collided with the system's innermost planet, reducing it to a fiery lump.

The collection of galactic garbage was then sucked into the windward side of the star, causing an epic coronal mass ejection on its leeward side.

A passing planet, in opposition to the catastrophe, caught the full brunt of the star's plasma storm, destroying its magnetic field and stripping it of its atmosphere. Unbeknownst to anyone, that victim had only just achieved the first stages of life.

None of this mattered to the sharpshooters aboard the *Collectors*. They were too busy enjoying a private celebration of their latest conquest.

The major was drinking his favorite cocktail, and conversing with his assistant, "Can you believe those fools on the Decronian Council tried to deny they owed payment? Blaming it on some rogue commander no less?"

The assistant smirked. "I guess they've got the message about tax laws now, haven't they?"

"Hmmm, I'm not sure the Earthlings will be pleased with the outcome. I assume, given they called us, the debt was significant, but screw them for failing to do their jobs in the first place.

"Once the *Ravager* returns, we'll deal with them, take what we can, and collect our bounty from the Americans."

A voice squawked through the ship's communications system, "*Ravager* sighted. All stations prepare for battle."

The *Unsympathetic Collectors'* array of weapons came to life. Blasters reduced the debris to rubble, and the rubble to drek. With a clear shot at their prey, the *Unsympathetic Collectors* honed their sights on the Decronian craft.

As for the *Ravager*, its firepower was no match. The advantage it held over the Federation ship was speed and maneuverability.

The photon beams burst from the *Collectors'* cannons.

Druote ordered, "180 Defensive Roll. Now!"

The maneuver was risky at best, a death move at worst. The G-force required not only to flip the *Ravager* over, but also to spin it in the opposite direction, had the potential to tear the seams of the spacecraft apart, imploding the ship.

No one on the bridge dared voice their fears as the *Ravager* groaned and crackled its displeasure at being forced to perform a feat for which it was not designed.

Fortune favored the crew. Although the occupants and cargo took a beating, the ship found itself facing the opposite direction, and the entrance to the wormhole.

Without needing the command, the navigator jumped into the dizzying tunnel's hyperspace, leaving the *Unsympa-*

thetic Collectors in their cosmic dust... literally and figuratively.

While the *Ravager* escaped through the wormhole, the crew scrambled to right the jumbled cargo, as well as any upended equipment.

Druote called down from the helm, "Jettison all cargo immediately. We need to lighten the ship as much as possible."

The Quartermaster replied, "That's impossible in the wormhole, sir. If we open the bay doors at this speed, we will dematerialize." Adding, as an afterthought, "Besides, interstellar littering is a Galactic crime punishable by no less than fifty—"

"Gods. I know the law, you fool."

Druote was left with an unpalatable alternative, but he had no choice. The order all but stuck in his throat. "Navigator, take us *back* to Earth. I refuse to be lumbered with those vermin."

Chapter 4

July 2, 2020
Hannson's Reach

Since the market for the bungalows and clapperboard cottages had opened, the Reach had become a destination for the wealthy hoi polloi, with Agnes' office earning more money than the three could imagine spending in a lifetime. Not even the threat of COVID could deter them.

Furthermore, the obscene amount of income — most of which the IRS had turned a blind eye to, partly to cover up the government's collusion in the debacle, and partly in exchange for the women's cooperation — went a long way towards ameliorating the suffering the women had endured after losing their families.

Agnes, for one, had convinced Joaquin to authorize an expansion of her home and surrounding property. Her Olympic-sized swimming pool with accompanying, ridiculously handsome, cabana boy, eased her *grief*.

The new residents had offered her the mayoral seat vacated by her husband; but she declined graciously, using the mountain of paperwork generated by filling the island with fresh faces as an excuse.

Deloris ended up dating and, subsequently, agreeing to marry the project's general contractor. Their wedding date was set for Valentine's Day the following year

As for Rochelle, she had turned her home into a B&B and moved back to the mainland. She was quick to embrace the concept of telecommuting, and returned to the Reach only when the need to show a property arose.

This Founders Day, as the island prepared for the annual observance, the island's trio of realtors were expecting formal notification from the Family Court that they were classed as widows with no encumbrances. It was seven years since their husbands had vanished without a trace.

Agnes Cheatham viewed the day with dread and relief. There were times she missed her husband, and not even Miguel could fill the hole. Nevertheless, she was a practical woman, and knew it was a waste of emotion to mourn his absence. Theirs was not the happiest of marriages.

Pushing everything else to the back of her mind, Agnes started her day by showing one of the last vacant properties on Hansson's Reach.

A couple from Portland, Oregon was excited to revamp what was once the island's only cafe, to open a franchise of a popular coffee chain. The fact, the upper floor housed a cozy apartment, made it even more enticing.

Descending the stairs, Agnes stopped midway to point out, "As you can see, we've worked hard to maintain a retro vibe in the booths and counter, while updating the amenities."

The couple traded glances, as through contemplating an unasked question.

Agnes was already ahead of them; she had heard the same question time and again. "No, no one died here. The spill did not cause any loss of life on the Reach, unless you consider the marine life in the surrounding fishing grounds, oh, and the fishing industry here as a whole. Those were the only true casualties.

"Like the rest of the island's population, the previous owner opted to leave rather than wait for the rehabilitation process to be completed."

She offered a smile. "The EPA did an incredible job clearing up the mess and regenerating the marine environment, which has encouraged the return of the sports fishermen who will need a good cup of coffee."

"There's no risk of disease from the waste?" the husband asked.

"I guarantee you have no reason to fear a return of any of the pollutants."

The man extended his hand to Agnes, "In that case, I think we have a deal."

"That's great, let's go to the office and draw up the paperwork."

After the contract was signed, Agnes decided to close the office early. A celebration awaited.

Along with Rochelle and Deloris, she had accepted a seat of honor on the VIP grandstand to watch the parade.

Sharing drinks, the women observed the crowds congregating along the street. The attendance was much lower than any of the three could recall. A sad reflection of the lack of community which once bound the inhabitants of Hansson's Reach.

The current residents shied away from their neighbors, preferring to bury their noses in some handheld device, texting the person across the table from them instead of conversing, and had no interest in the island's history.

As the sun slid towards the horizon, the boat parade began. Gone were the days of proudly decorated fishing trawlers, replaced by speed boats and cabin cruisers decorated with scantily clad women.

The Reach's high school band had suffered during the repopulation. Most of the new families either chose not to have children or homeschooled them. In the past, the school had boasted eighty children, most of whom were in the band now, there were less than thirty, and only a handful played an instrument.

The women, tasked with bringing the island to this point, watched the proceedings in silence applauding at relevant intervals.

As it had in the past, the sun played its part perfectly; the start of the fireworks signaled by the green shimmer on the edge of the horizon.

Propelled skywards, the first starburst exploded in a glittering shower of sparkles, increasing in brilliance when it reflected off the hull of the *DSS Ravager* as the spaceship descended from the upper atmosphere.

As though the sight of an unidentified flying object was not enough to cause mass panic what occurred next, incited total chaos, propelling the population in all directions as they bolted for cover.

Before the craft came to a complete stop, Druote commanded, "Jettison the cargo."

A blinding blue light flashed from beneath the *Ravager*, blanketing the island. Four hundred and ninety-seven life support pods were deposited haphazardly over the parade route, along the shoreline, into the ocean, onto the shiny new roofs, and through polished windows the length and breadth of the Reach.

The hold emptied of the excess weight, the ship's navigator thrust the *Ravager* back into upper orbit, in preparation to jump to the nearest friendly planet, but he never got the chance.

Waiting for the *DSS Ravager* was a force even more terrifying than the IRS. The Intergalactic Bureau of Investigation. Their ships encircled the vessel as it tried to flee, blocking its path.

A voice boomed over the *Ravagers* speakers, "*DSS Ravager,* stay where you are. This is agent 8259 of the IBI. You are under arrest for assorted tax crimes and illegal dumping…" the voice was suddenly muffled, as if a hand was placed over the microphone, but a conversation could be discerned.

"Do I really need to include that?" 8259 asked disdainfully of someone else aboard her ship.

Clearly, the response was in the affirmative. "Fine," the agent grumbled as she returned to address the crew of the *Ravager.* "And your navigator is under arrest for reckless piloting and speeding within a wormhole. Prepare to be boarded."

On the island, the pods burst open in unison. Those who survived the abandonment awoke slowly to find themselves in surroundings they struggled to recognize, and now an even larger problem loomed.

Chapter 5

In the two months since the return of the 433, as they became known, life had not come to a standstill.

With the indisputable proof that, for the last half-century, the conspiracy theorists were correct about the US government's complacency regarding numerous claims of alien abductions, the powers that be braced for the inevitable backlash.

Opinion among Americans had transitioned from fear of the unknown, through acceptance that they were not alone in the universe, to anger, along with demands for an armed revolution to punish the collaborators in Washington.

The outlook for the repatriated was grim. With nowhere to live — given their homes and properties had been confiscated by the IRS in lieu of outstanding government rates left unpaid at the time of their abduction — the returned were reduced to living in a tent city on the outskirts of the Reach.

The outlook for the repatriated was grim. Assorted, trumped up, taxes aside, their properties now belonged to the incomers, leaving them living like refugees in a tent city on the outskirts of the Reach.

This led to the filing of numerous court cases against the government and Agnes Cheatham's agency.

The current owners of the homes refused to relinquish possession of what they believed they had purchased legitimately, and the US government was hoping to write off the entire fiasco by claiming the plaintiffs were considered legally deceased under federal statutes for missing people and, as such, held no standing as US citizens.

As well as fighting off lawsuits from the previous inhabitants, the new owners had initiated proceedings against the IRS and Agnes for failure to disclose the truth behind the island's abductions, and fraud pertaining to the clean-up.

Exacerbating the unexpected overpopulation, every available inch of land left on the island was staked out by the various news outlets, desperate to cover the judicial circus.

Adding to the media frenzy, pundits from both ends of the political spectrum stormed about Hansson's Reach, fighting amongst themselves, ad nauseum, about rights and government responsibilities, but no one offered a viable solution.

Lest anyone forget the adage, *do not let a good disaster go to waste*, hawkers had set up shop selling novelty T-shirts, hats, and buttons in support of the *Ultimate Illegal Aliens*.

On top of this, Agnes's husband was suing her for divorce.

By sheer fluke, Wilbur Cheatham's pod crashed through the roof of his wife's newly constructed, redwood pergola, smashing the repository of expensive alcohol she had accrued in readiness to celebrate unwedded bliss. After clambering out of the rubble, amazed he was in one piece and more than a little disorientated, Wilbur was dumbfounded to find a naked cabana boy, who introduced himself as Miguel, lounging in a brand new pool.

To rub salt into an already gaping wound, Miguel offered

Wilbur a drink from the bottle he had appropriated from the aforementioned cache, before the wanton destruction, observing cheekily, "It appears you need this more than me."

As the truth of what had happened was revealed, Wilbur added these two 'discoveries' to what was becoming a hefty claim for compensation, in the amount of half of everything his wife had accumulated during an absence of which he had no recall.

Despite his best efforts, Agent Joaquin Navarro ended up in a courtroom to answer for the travesty in the Atlantic.

What began when the front door of his home was obliterated by an extra-large, forty-pound *key* — wielded by a proportionally sized muscle-head — followed by a questionable warrant, thrust into his hands stating the FBI's intention to acquire evidence proving Navarro was guilty of embezzlement, culminated in the ransacking of his house with extreme malice.

His furniture was overturned and sliced open needlessly. Drawers and cupboards searched with a fine-tooth comb, their contents strewn about.

The squad appeared to be putting an extra effort into disrupting his abode, probably to distract Joaquin from spotting two other agents making a beeline for his den.

It was only when he heard a small, controlled explosion, that he realized what they were up to.

The IRS and Feds needed a scapegoat. Their agent, the perfect patsy.

Although methodical in tracking expenditure during the restoration of Hansson's Reach, he had no plausible explanation for the account ledgers found in his private safe.

His defense. "Someone set me up."

An accusation his assistant — the venerable Ophelia Dulles who knew how the game was played, and on which side her bread was buttered — refuted under oath, "Your Honor, I saw my superior in possession of those files countless times. I was in no position to question him about their purpose, so I followed Service policy with diligence, and reported my concerns to the relevant authorities."

During an unscheduled recess, the prosecutor approached Joaquin with a one-time offer of either choosing to fight the charges and, as the man said, "Be guaranteed a thirty-year sentence in the recently opened federal penitentiary in Thomson, Illinois. You're familiar with that one, aren't you Agent Navarro. It's the one National Public Radio labeled the Deadliest Prison in America."

"Or?" Joaquin asked, certain the alternative was no less distasteful, just a shorter sentence.

"Or, plead guilty to all charges, and spend…" he paused to look at his fancy watch. "…let's say five years at Montgomery, Alabama's minimum-security prison. Who knows, with good behavior you could be out in eighteen months, with a sharpened tennis serve. Use the time to write your memoirs. I'm sure you could earn a buck or two from them."

It took less than a milli-second for Joaquin to order his new tennis racket.

Chapter 6

Mediating the civil cases were not as simple.

Some plaintiffs on either side of the ownership issue came to financial agreements with the federal government and chose to move on, while others elected to fight to the bitter end.

One was a returned citizen called Sprague, a widower whose wife, Cordelia, had passed twenty-some years ago and was buried in the community cemetery. They had bought adjoining plots, and he was determined to be buried next to her.

The house they once shared had been in Cordelia's family since 1839.

Sprague suffered from recurring dreams that she was rolling in her grave because strangers had taken up residence in her home and refused to be chased away despite her haunting them. In fact, this did nothing more than trigger a visit from annoying ghost hunters and a feature on the internet stream, *Phantom Trackers*.

The widower's case was taken up, pro bono, by a legal

team from New York, who wanted to enhance their reputation by standing up for the underdog.

The trial dragged on for weeks as the plaintiff and defendants submitted all manner of testimony through the courtroom.

It was a surprise witness, subpoenaed by the defense who flipped the case on its head.

Dressed in prison orange, which accentuated his chromium flesh, Commander Druote lumbered into the courtroom, ankles hobbled with heavy chains, and wrists secured to his torso with a body harness.

He was sworn in, electing to forgo the *So help me God* portion of the pledge. His own faith forbade him from recognizing any other gods but those of his former planet.

The bailiff asked him to state his name.

"Druote."

"Ah, is that your given name or family name?" The bailiff's brows knitted in confusion.

"Yes," Druote replied, making himself comfortable in the chair.

Despite the gravity of the hearing, a ripple of amusement drifted around the courtroom. The vague tension caused by the alien's hulking presence eased.

At a nod from the judge, proceedings continued. The defense lawyer, one Oliver Holmes V, rose to address the witness.

"Mister Druote—"

"That's Commander."

"Excuse me?" Holmes was momentarily nonplussed.

"Commander Druote of the Decronian commercial ship, *DSS Ravager*," Druote elaborated somewhat imperiously.

"Oh, of course, Commander," Holmes corrected himself. "Now, if you could answer a few questions.

"First, please confirm your previous occupation?"

"I was, as your people say, an exotic animal handler and exporter for the Council of Elders for my former planet of Decronia. As I have already told you, I am in command of the *DSS Ravager.*"

"*Former* planet?" Holmes quizzed curiously.

"Yeah, seems the Internal Revenue Service took offense over a few missed tax payments and had my home planet vaporized."

"I am sorry to hear that."

Druote shrugged at the sympathy, the gesture jingling his shackles.

"Moving along," Holmes continued. "What were your responsibilities in gathering these… exotic creatures?"

Druote scratched his chin meditatively. "We traveled the universe in search of beings suitable to take home to sell as pets or for zoo exhibits. Humans made some of the best profits. As a species, you really do make great pets."

"When was your last visit to our planet… down to the minute and second, if possible," Holmes asked.

"According to our ship's log, in Earth time, it would be twenty-one, oh-one, fifty-two, on oh-seven, oh-two: twenty-thirteen."

"And your return? Please be exact."

Oh seven, oh two: twenty-twenty," Druote replied curtly. "Some time around nine p.m."

"It is very important, Commander, that you remember precisely."

"I do not understand why it should and, anyway, I was too preoccupied with other things at the time to check my watch."

"It makes all the difference in the world, sir, as to whether or not the Returned can be deemed living or—"

Suddenly, Druote raised his palm to curb Holmes's questioning. The lawyer was so surprised he complied.

Placing a finger to his ear nub, Druote spoke in undertones, "Mhmm, I understand. I am pleased to hear—"

"Excuse me, Commander Druote," Holmes interrupted impatiently, not used to being ignored.

Druote repeated the gesture, this time accompanied by a menacing glare, and continued the muttered conversation, "No, no, you did exactly what I wanted. Proceed."

With that, Druote settled back, crossing his legs casually, his fingers tapping idly against the wooden arm as though in anticipation, although of what, none in the courtroom could fathom.

Holmes took this as a sign to press on but, before he could open his mouth, the brilliant blue beam the world had come to recognize burst through the ceiling of the courthouse.

A knowing smile spread across Druote's toothy mouth. Wryly, he informed the lawyer, and the rest of Earth, "Seems my erstwhile home was not the only place in this universe indebted to the galactic tax collectors.

"My crew informs me, your miniscule planet is about to be visited by a fleet of Federation Revenue Destroyers, seeking reimbursement for this whole fiasco and, since they cannot collect from Decronia, it appears Earth is picking up the check.

"Oh, and as the Decronian Council discovered, to their detriment, there's a substantial penalty for delinquent payment. Never mind, at least it will settle your current legal problems once and for all."

To the shock of the packed courtroom, the iridescent light encompassed the large figure who de-materialized in front of their eyes; a few words in the right ear securing Druote's escape.

The last anyone heard was a bellow of mocking laughter accompanied by his scathing farewell, "As you Earthlings are so fond of saying, Karma is a bitch!"

Consequences

Chapter 1

Jasper McCullin and Sanford Harman stood outside the Cambria City Bank, well-versed in the roles each would play in the next few minutes. A plan they had gone over time and again.

Jasper glanced through the window of the bank's door weighing up whether the two of them could handle the crowd. Meanwhile, Harman surveyed the length of the street for any sign of the sheriff or a wannabe town hero.

Satisfied, they nodded to one another, and pulled their bandanas up over their noses.

They had ridden in from the Dakota Territory a few days ago, choosing to camp out in the hills circling the town, so no one in Cambria would recognize them. The masks just added another level of anonymity.

The pair looked at each other, and Jasper used his fingers as a silent count down.

Three. Two. One.

They burst into the bank, yelling, "This is a hold up. One wrong move and you're dead."

That was when all hell broke loose.

Chapter 2

Jasper McCullin slumped on the bottom bunk of the single cell in Cambria's jail. The bang and creak of carpentry drifted through the barred window.

For the fifth time since sunrise, he stretched his legs and stood to peer through the window to watch the progress of the construction. It was the only source of entertainment the Wyoming territory company town had to offer.

McCullin was amazed at how quickly the framework was completed. He pictured the wooden beams being transformed into a hotel, something of which the town was in desperate need.

"You know darn well what they are building Jasper," a voice from the top bunk taunted.

Turning to confront the source of the aggravating comment, Jasper's eyes narrowed at the man stretched out on the top bunk, his hat covering his face.

"I don't need to hear anything from you, but for your stupidity, Harman, I wouldn't be in this mess," he spat gruffly. "So, shut your trap already. I swear to God my ears are about to bleed out."

For the better part of the night, the two men had argued back and forth over who was more to blame for the bungled bank robbery.

Harman chuckled. "Can't see how any of this could possibly be on me? I was just followin' your plan."

Cambria was under the strict control of Kilpatrick Brothers and Collins, the company which, as well as being contractors to the Chicago, Burlington & Quincy Railroad, owned the town in its entirety, along with everything connected to it, including the mine.

To ensure compliance and reduce any chance of the drunken fracas plaguing other mining towns, saloons and brothels were forbidden, and the company had introduced its own monetary script, without which purchases were impossible.

This made Cambria a prime target for hold ups because incomers were compelled to transfer any cash into company dollars.

"Explain to me how that damn bank guard got the drop on you with his shotgun?"

"Born lucky, I guess."

"Bah, if you had stuck to the plan, we would have been in and out before anybody noticed," Jasper snapped, "but here we are, me staring up at your ugly face, and you just lazin' around like it's a Sunday afternoon picnic. The least you could do is come up with a plan to get me out of here."

"Nope, not my job. You're the planner, remember. I'm just the hired gun," Harman contested.

"Yeah, stupid of me to forget you weren't in line the day the Lord dished out brains." Jasper groused.

"Hey, if we're gonna throw insults, who was the idiot who shot the teller?"

"What was I supposed to do? The fool pulled a gun."

"You could have run. That's what I would have done, hindsight being what it's worth."

"And leave you there to fend for yourself?" Jasper felt a twinge of regret, despite the flash of clarity telling him self-preservation was, indeed, the better alternative.

Harman chuckled. "Your heroics didn't amount to a hill o' beans, did they."

"All the same, I'm sorry for getting you involved in this mess."

"Pfft, wouldn't have missed it for the world."

Chapter 3

The bang of nails into wood ended abruptly, followed by the thud of boots and the metallic squawk of a lever being yanked. The twang of a rope, and the whoosh of something heavy falling, informed anyone nearby that the gallows was set for its guest.

The loud jangle of keys jerked Jasper's attention from the window to the door of his cell.

The sheriff was fiddling with the lock. Beside him stood one of his deputies, armed with a Winchester Model 1873 .44-40 rifle, just in case the prisoner decided to make a run for it.

That thought *had* crossed Jasper's mind. Perhaps a bullet in the back was preferable to what awaited him.

As though Harman had read his thoughts, he swung himself upright, letting his legs dangle from the top bunk, then jumped down.

Jasper watched as his accomplice landed on his feet, which, oddly, emitted no sound.

Harman leaned towards Jasper. "Time to man up, partner," he rasped.

Studying Harman closely, Jasper registered a couple of unsettling details he had not noticed until this moment. Firstly, his hat sat lower on his head than usual. Secondly, there was a dark bloodstain around the brim.

Stepping back, Harman smiled and tipped his hat. Jasper gawked as nausea swamped him. The top half of his friend's head was missing. Not only had the guard beaten Harman to the draw but also, he had blown his fool skull apart, eyes and all.

For the better part of the night, Jasper had conversed with a dead man.

Returning the hat to the stump of his head, Harman nodded and walked straight through the sheriff, who shivered. The latter glanced around seeking the source of the chill, but saw nothing to explain it.

Shrugging it off, he removed the cuffs from his belt, and secured Jasper's wrists behind him.

Satisfied the prisoner was not going to escape, he informed Jasper in a voice devoid of emotion, "It's time."

When Jasper McCullin left his cell to take the deadman's walk to the hangman's noose, he heard Harman say, "Don't worry, friend. We will meet up in Hell soon enough."

Uneasy Truce

Chapter One

West Flanders,
6th June 1917

Heads turned skyward at the sound of the lone bi-plane circling above the scorched remains of the once beautiful forest. Binoculars on both sides glinted in the afternoon sun as their owners attempted to identify the nationality of the craft.

The German division needed no second guesses to pinpoint its origin when, seconds later, two grenades dropped six hundred feet into their heavily manned trenches.

Pleased with his aim, the pilot crowed, "See that? Sent 'em scurryin' like mice at the sight of the cat.

Lead projectiles from the enemy's front line filled the sky in an attempt to bring down the makeshift bomber.

Assuming the racket from the German's signalled a charge, the Allies answered with a ferocious volley of artillery to thwart the suspected advance.

High above, the man in the rear seat of the aircraft was

less than impressed by the sudden engagement his partner had precipitated.

Instead of a congratulatory whoop from Léon, photographer and reluctant passenger, Willy received a solid whack to the back of his head.

"Goddammit, Willy, you know the rules. We are only up here to observe and take photographs, not get shot down by a stray bullet because you want to be a war hero," Léon berated.

"Bah," Willy bristled. "They'll need somethin' bigger than those cheap German rifles to bring us down."

Jabbing a finger at the destroyed vegetation beneath them, Willy yelled, "Shit, it took a mighty barrage of shells to fell them trees. Ain't no way any of those turkey shooters gonna hit us."

Willy was reiterating his pledge to keep Léon safe, when a couple of bullets whizzed through the canvas skin of their wing.

A third tore straight through the rear cockpit, barely missing Léon's thigh, leaving him with one decision — ignore Willy and finish their assignment.

The reconnaissance images of the battlefield below would not take themselves, and the pair could not return to the security of the aerodrome and, more importantly, a waiting pint or two of beer, without filling the reel.

Closing his ears to Willy's bluster, Leon looked through the camera viewer. A fierce frown marred his brow.

The zigzagging trenches resembled ugly, putrid wounds left by the careless slashes of some monstrous beast.

While Gaia's resilience might heal the Earth, I am sure man has inflicted so much damage to the ridge it will never recover.

What rent Léon's heart more deeply were the memories of his grandfather taking him to explore these very woods, which once ran from Wytschaete to Zonnebeke, when he was a child. Trees he used to climb stood gnarled and twisted, their trunks, tangled with barbed wire, were broken and blackened from the intense bombardments.

Pushing aside melancholy thoughts, he steeled himself to zoom in on any manoeuvres unfolding along the tortuous lines, however insignificant they might seem from this distance, as best he could.

The Germans were business as usual, dying in droves, more from malnutrition and dysentery than the unrelenting barrages inflicted by the opposition.

Flemish born and bred, Léon was dismissive of his American counterparts, especially this idiot of a pilot, but the allied forces beneath him had earned his respect.

He pressed the shutter, capturing images of the clash unfurling below.

"Such a waste. We will run out of cannon fodder before we run out of bullets," Léon muttered, uncaring whether the buffoon in the front seat was listening.

He gained a modicum of relief when, zooming the lens to its furthest extent, he spotted allied servicemen pressed against the earthen walls of the trenches in a desperate attempt to find refuge. That the grenades had landed among the enemy, offered little comfort. Neither was it of any solace that, from this altitude, he could not see the fear he knew must be etched on their faces.

No doubt someone will invent a camera before long with a lens sharp enough to capture the souls of soldiers as they detach from their mortal coils.

Léon scanned the Allied lines, catching sight of ladders rising from the depths.

God, no. Please stop this insanity.

The only reply to his disconsolate plea was the blast of a whistle echoing over the din of battle as though Gabriel's trumpet was heralding the rapture.

Furiously snapping photographs, Léon watched the troops pour over the top into the devastated woodland. Scrambling across the ground, dropping behind whatever protection they came across, whether that be a stump, a mound of dirt, or the corpse of a fallen comrade.

Slapping Willy on the shoulder, Léon snagged the pilot's attention. Gesticulating frantically, he motioned for Willy to bank the plane over the German lines.

His stomach knotted, as his suspicions were confirmed. Under the intensity of German Maschinengewehr 08 machine guns, the enemy infantry was responding in kind.

Merde, all this thanks to the imbecile in front of me. I hope the ghosts of every one of these men haunt his dreams for the rest of his life.

Watching dirt spray in all directions as exploding mortars gouged deadly craters into the landscape, all Léon could do was finish his own mission.

Chapter Two

While most of the occupants in the trench were fixated on the circling Dorand AR.2 biplane, Lance Corporal Whitaker Crafton of the 3rd Australian Division of the Second Anzac Corps, had lost interest in the elaborate aerobatics long since.

After months of sloshing through the mud of the various Allied front line trenches, the freedom the sky offered the Army Air Corps was a cruel taunt.

It compounded Crafton's aggravation with everything related to this accursed war, the airborne soldiers becoming the latest to bear the brunt of his frustration, despite the fact they were on the same side.

Another platform from which men can kill each other, although being up there, they might end up in heaven a few seconds earlier than those dying around me.

The son of devoted Quakers, Crafton grew up outside Sydney, New South Wales, his religious beliefs qualifying him to file for Conscientious Objector status.

When Crafton reported for duty, he was ordered to present himself to his commanding officer. Standing at attention in front of the Colonel's desk, Crafton was at a loss as to the reason for the summons.

To be enlightened immediately.

"Look, son, I don't know why the hell—" the C.O. stopped himself and cleared his throat. "I'm not sure why recruiters continue to send your kind to my division, but I have no room for anyone not prepared to take a life when needed. I suggest, no, I strongly recommend you reconsider your position. I shall not think any less of you for remaining true to your religious convictions."

Crafton did not hesitate, "Sir, while I believe this war is an unnecessary travesty foisted upon humanity because of the selfish whims of petty European potentates, I cannot countenance someone going in my stead."

That answer appeared to convince the C.O. and, once his uniform was dispensed, Crafton became the, not so proud, possessor of a short magazine Lee Enfield Mark lll rifle, complete with a Pattern 1907 bayonet and a canvas kit bag brim-full of Mark VI ball ammunition.

Even after Crafton, who had fought in and survived the Gallipoli campaign, landed on French soil, the Australian Imperial Force seemed intent on keeping him on the periphery. He was offered a non-combatant's role of medical corpsman, which — after due consideration… all of thirty seconds — he rejected. The notion of running around the battlefield, unarmed, was less attractive than carrying a weapon.

The soldier next to him on the transport train to the front, nodded his head at Crafton's Enfield rifle and shrugged a pump-action shotgun off his shoulder, handing it to Crafton before the latter could demur.

"Take a look at this. Ain't she a beauty? You should ask your folks to send you one. Those pig stickers are fine and all, but my scatter gun will kill five times as many Huns before you've even raised your rifle."

Crafton examined the weapon, noting the Winchester manufacturer's stamp on the blue steel. The barrel was shorter than the average gun — twenty inches max, he guessed.

"The nine load 00 buckshot cartridge will tear through flesh, and guarantees they won't be getting up," said the soldier, whose soft drawl suggested he might be a Canadian, then changed tack. "Don't suppose you have a smoke?"

Smoking was a habit Crafton's mother did not condone but, circumstances being what they were, he reckoned what she did not know would not hurt her.

Digging out his half-empty packet, Crafton handed the cigarettes to the soldier, watching him tap one out, put it between his lips, and pocket the rest.

Crafton debated whether to protest the loss, as the stranger lit the cigarette and drew on it, the tip flaring red. Exhaling a cloud, he introduced himself.

"Name's Jackson, but everyone calls me Mooch. Not sure why. Fresh from Toronto by way of Swindon." He winked. "Ma is from London. You an Aussie?"

Returning the shotgun to his new *friend*, and pleased he had picked the accent, Crafton felt obliged to reciprocate, and extended his hand. The man had not clarified whether Jackson was his first or last name, and Crafton was not interested enough to pry. "I am, and nice to meet you, Mooch. I'm Whitaker Crafton."

"That's a mouthful, bud. Mind if I shorten it to Whit."

"No worries." Crafton shrugged carelessly.

The deep, grumbling voice of their sergeant barked, "If you two are done with your tea party, I suggest you report to your respective barracks before I decide I need a couple of latrines dug before lunch."

Mooch shook his head and whispered to Crafton as he hoisted his pack, "Stick with me, Whit. I'll make sure you don't go without and, more importantly, that you're on the transport back to Australia when this is over."

True to his word, Mooch stuck to Crafton like glue, which the latter found irritating but could not deny that Mooch, when they were on rotation, always managed to procure decent wine, the least objectionable places to rest one's head and very hospitable women.

From Crafton's first encounter with the Germans, he curbed his tongue and let the Canadian tag along.

Late afternoon, 6th June 1917
West Flanders

In the sinuous network of earthworks, tension ran high among the men, most just desperate to get it over with. Oddly, more often than not, the waiting was worse than the actual engagement.

The objective of this major offensive, the preparations for which had been months in the making, was to neutralise a series of German defences stretching along a ridge from Ploergsteeert Wood to Mount Sorrel giving them a strategic, high-ground position from where they could virtually see into the Allies' trenches.

At a signal, a barrage of artillery began followed by the usual wave of soldiers scrambling over the top into no man's land, firing remorselessly to weaken the German's fortifications.

The enemy's Mauser Gewehr 98 rifles, accompanied by

the remorseless rat-tat-tat of their MG 08 machine, spewed a wall of death at the advancing allies.

Despite those around them being felled by the relentless gunfire, neither Crafton nor Mooch slowed their charge or returned fire.

Reaching cover, the pair dropped to their knees and took aim.

Crafton's shot caught the forward German gunner in the throat, toppling him over his MG 08, while Mooch pumped shell after shell of his deadly buckshot into the bodies of anyone in grey who dared step into his sights.

As ever, the engagement resulted in too many men lying dead or dying in no man's land,

While generals patted each other on the back, medics scuttled up and down their respective trenches in a desperate bid to save any who had crawled back into their muddy hell.

The seriously injured were evacuated through the complex chain of aid posts, clearing stations, and hospitals which straggled out from the rear of the trench network. The walking wounded were patched up and sent back to the lines, the dead were moved when it was convenient.

One who made it to the relative safety of the trench was Crafton, carrying Mooch. His sidekick had learned the hard way that the human anatomy was not built to stop a German bayonet counterattack.

In the confusion, Mooch had ended up ahead of Crafton. By the time the latter caught up, he found his friend bleeding profusely from a grievous wound to his abdomen.

Seeing Crafton illuminated by the flares and exploding projectiles, Mooch reached out a trembling hand. Coughing up blood, he begged, "Please don't leave me to die in this filth."

Hefting Mooch onto his back, Crafton instructed him to, "Hang on, mate," then zigzagged across the field in a mad and risky dash.

In sight of safety, he felt Mooch's grip slacken and heard him whisper, "I-I'm sorry, y-you're on your own," as he slithered to the soiled earth.

Determined to get to the trench, he grabbed Mooch by his gun and, dragging him the last twenty yards by its strap, hauled him over the edge.

Landing with a squelch, Crafton called for a medic, and checked for a pulse, knowing it was futile. He could not help himself; it was something the living did for the dead, just in case.

Exhausted and heartsore, Crafton slumped next to the corpse and buried his face in his hands, unable to stem the tears for the annoying idiot who had called him friend.

Unhooking Mooch's gun from his body, Crafton promised, "I'll see this is returned to your folks."

Once he secured it on his back, he scooped Mooch out of the mud before the rats descended.

His attention on the ruined corner of a wall which acted as the aid station, Crafton elbowed his way past a couple of soldiers who were comparing shrapnel wounds, too occupied with debating whether this was enough to get them sent home to notice Crafton.

The scent of cold, damp earth, and death assaulted his nostrils. Lying Mooch on a canvas cloth which seemed suited to the purpose, and unaware of the protocols, he yelled at one of the orderlies, "See he is sent home in decent condition, or I'll drag you out to No Man's Land and dump you there."

His plea fell on deaf ears. The dead had no say here; the priority of the hardy medics was for those clinging to life.

Chapter Three

June 6th 1917

The sudden silence from the battlefield encouraged Infanterist, Jakob Nussbaum, to peek over the top of the German trench to see corpsmen ascend their ladders like ants spilling out of their hills.

Red crosses displayed prominently on white armbands, distinguished them against the barren landscape as they scrambled to rescue the wounded.

Observing stretcher bearers worming through the barbed wire and checking mud-filled craters frantically trying to recover as many of their comrades as possible was akin to a game of chance, spawning macabre wagers as to how many could be retrieved before the rat-tat-tat of the guns scattered them back to their trenches

Nussbaum refused to participate in such shenanigans. The gamble they were taking with their lives already was bad enough.

Three Years Previously

Along with a hundred thousand of his Jewish brethren, Nussbaum had hurried to enlist after Kaiser Wilhelm's stirring speech of nationalistic pride and his invocation of God's defense of Germany delivered on 1ˢᵗ August 1914.

Even if this meant leaving the Heidelberger Juristische Fakultät and the final year of his law degree because, as the Kaiser proclaimed, "We shall, with God's help, so wield the sword that we shall restore it to its sheath again with honour."

The following day when Nussbaum reported to the trains heading for the military camp outside Munich, the platform of Heidelberg's railway station was crowded. He elbowed his way past young men who, dressed in their best suits, kissed wives or girlfriends farewell, promising to be home for Christmas.

The recruiters had guaranteed it.

Quick victories bolstered the troops, reinforced by claims that *Paris was but forty days away*. This rousing battle cry reverberated among those awaiting deployment in support of the advanced stormtroopers, along with jokes about purloining the finest French wine and clothing as gifts for their womenfolk.

Nussbaum's battalion chased the retreating British Expeditionary Force following the Battle of Mons. The morale of the British soldiers had taken a hit as word of their commanding officers' discontent with their French allies filtered down to the ranks.

A lieutenant in Nussbaum's company boasted to his men, that the Kaiser's generals were set to push the Tommies all the way to the Channel and back to England, outlining their part in the campaign.

Oberleutnant Gotfried Meyer stood in front of a hand-drawn map. "As you can see, gentlemen..." he smacked his pointer on the paper with a smart snap to emphasise the amount of French territory already under German control, "...the combined forces of the British and French have fled almost two hundred and fifty kilometres, in fear of our military might.

"We are tasked with flanking their retreat, with the aim of destroying their forces once and for all, then Paris will be ours for the taking."

A cheer erupted in the tent.

"We march in the morning," Meyer ordered the troops. "Victory is within reach!"

Laughter and hope of an early success came to an abrupt halt on the Marne River, twenty-five miles from the City of Lights. The allies, straightening their backbone, drove the German line back towards the Belgian border, where the battle stagnated into the quagmire of trench warfare.

For the next two years, the opposing sides traded the same narrow swathe of land countless times.

Late afternoon, 6th June 1917
West Flanders

For Jakob Nussbaum, and others of his faith, the period between 1915 and 1917 was not kind.

The Kaiser's general staff had convinced him that the stalemate on the Western Front was the fault of Germany's

Jewish community. The generals claimed most were dodging their military responsibilities or, were too lazy to be good soldiers.

His advisors suggested prohibiting the Jews from holding any rank above Oberleutnant in the front-line army, relegating Jewish officers to reservist units.

In a similar vein, a pay discrepancy which persisted between Jewish and non-Jewish soldiers was studiously ignored by the powers that be.

For Nussbaum, the lustre of patriotism had long since dulled.

No speech, however stirring, delivered by bombastic generals flaunting glittering, *battle won* medals, compensated for the catastrophic loss of lives for the sake of what amounted to — in the most simplistic terms, and complex system of alliances aside — a family squabble between three cousins: Kaiser Wilhelm II, King George V, and Tsar, Nicholas II.

The elite and their temper tantrums, Nussbaum thought as he peered over the edge of the trenches. *I would love to see any one of them spend the night with us in this hell. The war would be over in a heartbeat.*

"Damn you, Victoria for not being able to keep your damned knees together," Nussbaum grumbled under his breath, knowing better than to express his opinion any louder, for fear of being charged with treason.

Shrugging off mutinous thoughts, Nussbaum leaned against the crumbling dirt of the trench wall.

A sonorous drone shattered the almost reverent hush which inevitably descended on no man's land during the retrieval of the wounded, and he raised his eyes skyward. A trio of German Albatros D.IIIs had appeared from a cloud bank, catching the French reconnaissance biplane, from where the grenades had rained down earlier, unawares.

The pilot of the Dorand AR.2 showed his skill, avoiding the hail of lead from the German biplanes' Spandau machine guns with some nifty manoeuvres, simultaneously returning fire.

Unfortunately, given the angle of the German fighters' attack, any projectiles which missed or passed through their target, strafed the German lines, prompting men to scatter in all directions to avoid death by friendly fire.

Wearied by the dogfight, and disappointed he was not hit by stray fire, Nussbaum lit a cigarette and made himself comfortable.

Half-dozing, he was jolted awake by the harsh sputter of a critically damaged engine. Shielding his eyes against the sun, Nussbaum watched in impotent horror as the propellor on one of the aerial combatants shuddered and stalled, the dying whine of the motor unmistakable. In slow motion, almost lazily, the aircraft rotated, righted itself, then fell into a deadly tailspin.

Expecting the victim to be the French plane, suffering defeat at hands of the trio of seasoned German pilots, Nussbaum was shocked to register that it was one of the three Albatros' screaming its smoking downwards spiral.

The unavoidable demise of the plane ought to have spelled death to its occupant but, all credit to the pilot who drew on every ounce of his skill to fight the odds, and turned a catastrophic crash into an ungainly belly flop.

Regrettably, that was where his luck ran out. His lap belt jammed effectively pinning him inside the flaming wreckage.

The large target on the edge of the battlefield drew a volley of gunfire from the Allied side whose bullets raked the stricken plane, earning a return salvo from the Germans.

Caught in the crossfire, the pilot's pitiful pleas for help

went unheeded by the beleaguered stretcher bearers who, keeping low, made a beeline for safety with as many of their wounded as they had managed to rescue.

Acknowledging that what he was about to do was a fool's mission, Nussbaum could not sit back and watch the pilot die. At this point the mutual fusillade was not an act of war, but blatant murder.

Scaling the wall of the German trench, he ran to the plane yelling, "Shut up, dummkopf. Stop attracting attention. Let them think you dead."

His advice went unheard.

When Nussbaum reached the plane, the pilot was peppered with bullets. Resting his hand on the still warm corpse, he bowed his head in despair at the loss of a man he never knew.

About to retrace his impulsive dash, Nussbaum heard the chatter of machine guns and broke into a run.

Too late.

A fragment tore through his femur, leaving a white hot pain in its wake. His leg buckled, throwing him into the gore-soaked mud.

Agony robbing him of breath, Nussbaum tried to gage the distance between where he lay and the safety of his trench.

Uninjured, he might make it, but with a gaping hole in his leg, and bleeding profusely, he reckoned the odds were against him. Self-preservation told him his best bet was to crawl to the nearest crater and pray for a miracle.

Chapter Four

From the relative safety of his trench, Crafton watched the German drag himself to the crater. He did not know whether he ought to be impressed by the enemy's bravery for trying to save his compatriot, or brand him an idiot for risking his life in such a foolhardy manner.

What he *did* know was that to leave a wounded man, enemy or not, to die alone in an open grave went against everything he was ever raised to believe.

Slinging his rifle over one shoulder, Crafton spotted and grabbed a stray medical kit. He had one foot on the bottom rung of the closest ladder when he was halted by someone gripping his belt.

It was his sergeant. The grizzled man, battle-worn and weary, barked at the Quaker, "Where in the hell do you think you're going?"

"There's an injured man out there. Someone has to save him."

"Is he wearing olive drab or kraut grey?" the sergeant bit out.

"Does it matter? An injured man is an injured man no matter the nationality. Besides, aren't we supposed to be the *good guys* in this war?"

"Don't test me, soldier."

"I can't just leave someone out there to die, especially since he risked his life trying to save that pilot's—"

The sergeant looked at the downed aircraft and snorted. "You mean that bullet-riddled corpse still buckled into his cockpit?"

Swinging his steely gaze back to Crafton, he was startled to realize the corporal was no longer there. A glimpse over the top revealed a tall, lanky soldier dodging a renewed hail of gunfire, this time from the German side.

Crafton bobbed and wove the best he could. His comrades yelled at him to get his bloody stupid arse back to their trench, while the Germans bellowed from the other side. Crafton guessed it was probably along the lines of, "Kill him before he gets to Nussbaum."

He was within a few hundred yards, when the German's released another volley. Instantly answered by the Allies.

Can they not see how futile this is?

He reeled like a drunken sailor somehow avoiding the mortars exploding around him, until his luck ran out and one launched him off his feet into the pit.

He landed on the German, precipitating another confrontation.

Nussbaum struggled to push the stranger off him. He had no idea what the enemy soldier was saying presuming it was an order to surrender.

A command he refused to heed. Nussbaum had heard horror stories about the heinous tortures the Allies inflicted on German POWs in their rat-infested camps. He had seen posters of their doctors gouging eyes out of men's heads with metal tongs, while they were still awake.

Not to mention rumours of perverse medical experiments these same surgeons performed on their prisoners without the benefit of chloroform for no reason, except they had, literally, a captive audience.

Even if he was bleeding to death from his shattered leg, he was not succumbing to his injuries without sending this teufelshunde back to Hell and its master.

Crafton was trying to calm the man down so he could evaluate his wound. Risking an approach, he jerked back when the German drew his Nahkampfmesser from its sheath, and jabbed it menacingly.

Ever the Quaker, Crafton preferred not to do the same with his own trench knife but the enemy soldier left him no choice.

As Crafton's hand closed around the wooden grip, the German's blade came up, aiming to eviscerate his supposed attacker. Quick as lightning, the Australian blocked the attempt, landing a jagged punch to the soldier's face with his knife's built-in brass knuckles.

Nussbaum saw stars and blood spurted from his nose. While Crafton did not intend his blow to be quite so savage, in the face of the German's frenzy, he had no alternative.

"Stop," he bawled at the man, and pointed at the medical kit, following up with a poorly pronounced, "Halt, Aufhören. Genug."

Stop and enough were the only words he could remember from his German grandmother, instructions accompanied by a clip around the ear whenever Crafton did something of which she did not approve.

Nussbaum canted his head for a split second, trying to comprehend what the crazy soldier who had jumped into the crater was trying to tell him.

By dint of pointing at the red cross on his medical bag, accompanied by a series of mimes, and a bizarre mix of German and English, Crafton convinced the wounded soldier, he meant him no harm.

"Crafton." He indicated himself when, eventually, the German, wearied from blood loss and fear, stopped jabbing the wicked knife in his face.

"Nussbaum," the wounded man rasped, his face pinched and waxy, the pain in his leg reaching epic proportions.

Aware the artillery would continue unabated for several hours, Crafton was under no illusion about their chances of escaping this crater. He knew what was planned, all the allied soldiers on the ridge knew what was planned. His faith refused to let him relinquish a sliver of hope, while common sense urged him to pray it was quick.

As the sun began its slow descent to the horizon, the sky glowed dark red. A storm was in the offing.

It would be a long night.

As dusk fell, in the Allied Command post a judicious distance from the front line, the press was given the latest information regarding the imminent and massive offensive, a sure sign the powers that be were confident of its success.

During the preceding fifteen months, British Royal Engineers, along with Canadian, New Zealand, and Australian forces, had constructed a network of tunnels under Messines Ridge, approximately eighty to one hundred and twenty feet below the surface with the horizontal passages extending for over three miles under the German's front line.

The enemy had employed the same tactic, except their tunnels were not as deep, which the British had countered by digging a series of dummy tunnels at the same depth to camouflage their strategy and halt the German advance.

Once completed, the Allies filled their tunnels with nigh on a thousand tons of ammonal explosives and flammable gun cotton.

General Sir Charles Harrington, Chief of Staff of the Second Army announced to his listeners, "Gentlemen, I don't know whether we are going to make history tomorrow but, at any rate, we shall change geography."

As though in warning of what was to come, lightning rent the sky and thunder rumbled, while hardy war correspondents rushed to wire the details to their various offices with promises of more to follow.

The commanders held their breath and, by midnight, the sky had cleared allowing British aircraft to buzz the German lines to mask the growl of tanks rolling into position.

At the faint lessening of the darkness... first light came early at this time of the year... the rattle of artillery stopped. In the silence, the trill of birds welcoming the false dawn was at heartbreaking odds with the scene.

At 3:10 a.m., it began.

The mines were detonated at twenty second intervals,

When making their calculations, the Engineers had not counted on the sheer magnitude of the explosions. A mountain of dirt and mud erupted skywards, along with ten thousand German soldiers. On the Allied side, men were deafened by the percussion, which was heard in London and Dublin.

Decades into the future, historians compared it with the atomic blasts which obliterated Hiroshima and Nagasaki.

In a lonely artillery crater, two injured men barely had time to see the earth rent itself asunder before the debris rained down mercilessly, burying them alive.

Rori Bleu & Rosie Chapel

Success came at a very high price.

126

Epilogue

It was another seventeen months before the conflict came to an end. Four long years during which countless lives were lost for what appeared, to the rank and file on both sides, to be extraordinarily little gain.

In November 1918 an armistice was declared. Not peace exactly but, to the relief of all involved, a cessation of hostilities, which, thankfully, paved the way for the signing of the Treaty of Versailles on June 28, 1919.

Kaiser Wilhelm fled to the Netherlands, leaving others to clean up his mess.

Broken and bankrupt, Germany bore the brunt of the war, their financial and global humiliation brought the country to its knees

In a quiet corner of France, the blighted ridge which had claimed the lives of Lance Corporal Whitaker Crafton and Infanterist Jakob Nussbaum, was reclaimed by nature — as best as Gaia was able to heal the damage man had inflicted on her sovereign territory.

Regrettably, man never allows the dead slumber for long.

A mere twenty years after the *war to end all wars*, the ground trembled as an even more destructive force headed west under orders from Berlin to rectify the injustice imposed on German Nationalism.

Two spirits perched on the edge of the almost forgotten battlefield looked at each other, shaking their spectral heads in disbelief.

It took death for the erstwhile foe to find a common language and an uneasy truce. A tentative reconciliation, which those who still drew breath had yet to discover, and could be discerned only when enemies paused long enough to listen.

Until sense prevailed, the voices of countless brave souls who made the ultimate sacrifice were lost to the silence.

Rori Bleu

With a smattering of riverboat pirates and royalty in her
heritage, Rori Bleu's childhood reflected her past.
An interest in fairy tales, myth and legend were as important
as spirited discussions around politics and current affairs —
although some might argue they are one and the same!

A fascination, sparked by listening to Grimm's Fairy Tales at
her grandmother's knee, not only encouraged Rori's passion
for reading, but also steered her into the world of RPG's.
What began as a fun pastime, soon evolved into the creation
of fantastical worlds, but Rori never lost her love of politics
going on to specialise in Governmental History and
Historical Research.

Naturally this means her stories are steeped in historical
accuracy and real-life intrigue. While Rori's love of a happily
ever after means her preferred genre is romance, don't be
surprised if you discover an occasional detour into historical
fiction, thrillers, horror and fantasy.

Roșie Chapel

Rosie Chapel lives in Perth, Australia, with her hubby and two rescue fur babies. When not writing, she loves catching up with friends, burying herself in a book (or three), discovering the wonders of Western Australia, or — and the best — a quiet evening at home with her husband, enjoying a glass of wine and a movie.

Website: www.rosiechapel.com

Also by Rori Bleu

Pineapple Meringue

Imprisoned Hearts

Port of London

Dani's Masquerade

Black Tulips

Ajei's Destiny

Porta Aeternum

The Queen's Heart

Syn *with Matthew Forester*

With Rosie Chapel

Tapestry of Shadows and Light - The Hunters Prequel

Echoes and Illusions - The Hunters: Book 1

Smoke and Mirrors - The Hunters : Book 2

Evie's War

Vindicta

Corrupt Covenant

Lesser of Two Evils

Deadly Incision

The Sela Helsdatter Saga

A Flip of The Coin - Book One

Conceived Chaos - Book Two

Odin's Bane - Book Three

Valhalla's Doom - Book Four

Arcane Alchemy: Freya's Fate - *A Helsdatter Saga Novella*

Also by Rosie Chapel

<u>Historical Fiction</u>

The Hannah's Heirloom Sequence
The Pomegranate Tree - Book One
Echoes of Stone and Fire - Book Two
Embers of Destiny - Book Three
Etched in Starlight - Prequel
Hannah's Heirloom Trilogy - Compilation — e-book only

Prelude to Fate
Legacy of Flame and Ash

The Nettleby Trilogy (WW1 Novellas)
A Guardian Unexpected - Book One
Under the Clock - Book Two
Between Heartbeats - Book Three

<u>Regency Romances</u>
The Linen and Lace Series
Once Upon An Earl - Book One
To Unlock Her Heart - Book Two
Love on a Winter's Tide - Book Three
A Love Unquenchable - Book Four
A Hidden Rose — Book Five

An Unexpected Romance
Elusive Hearts - Book One

Shrouded Hearts - Book Two

The Daffodil Garden

The Unconventional Duchess

Rescuing Her Knight - *the de Wiltons:* Book One

His Fiery Hoyden

A Regency Duet

A Regency Christmas Double

Fate is Curious

A Christmas Prayer *with Ashlee Shades*

The Lady's Wager

Winning Emma

A Love Impossible

Unravelling Roana

Love Kindled

Moonbeams and Mistletoe

<u>Fairy Tale Romance</u>

Chasing Bluebells

<u>Contemporary Romances</u>

Of Ruins and Romance

All At Once It's You

Cobweb Dreams

Just One Step

His Heart's Second Sigh

With Rori Bleu

Tapestry of Shadows and Light - The Hunters Prequel

Echoes and Illusions - The Hunters: Book 1

Smoke and Mirrors - The Hunters : Book 2

Evie's War

Vindicta

Corrupt Covenant

Lesser of Two Evils

Deadly Incision

The Sela Helsdatter Saga

A Flip of The Coin - Book One

Conceived Chaos - Book Two

Odin's Bane - Book Three

Valhalla's Doom - Book Four

Arcane Alchemy: Freya's Fate - *A Helsdatter Saga Novella*

9 781763 775350